Emma M. Hooper

Home Dressmaking Made Easy

Volume 1

Emma M. Hooper

Home Dressmaking Made Easy
Volume 1

ISBN/EAN: 9783337391775

Printed in Europe, USA, Canada, Australia, Japan

Cover: Foto ©Andreas Hilbeck / pixelio.de

More available books at **www.hansebooks.com**

HOME DRESSMAKING MADE EASY.

BY

EMMA M. HOOPER,

*One of the Associate Editors of the "Ladies' Home Journal,"
and a member of the staff of the "Dry
Goods Economist."*

WITH ILLUSTRATIONS BY

ABBY E. UNDERWOOD.

NEW YORK :
THE ECONOMIST PRESS
1896.

CONTENTS.

INTRODUCTION.

The trite saying that "a dressmaker is born, not made" cannot hold good in these days when so many conveniences are offered to the non-professional in the way of dress systems, patterns, etc. The great majority of women are of what is styled "middle-class circumstances" and they must become dressmakers for themselves or very often go without a new gown.

A desire to be well dressed is inborn with every woman, and man as well, and why not follow this desire unless it cause one to neglect home duties or induces one to spend more than can be afforded upon one's wardrobe? When neatly and becomingly attired a woman is happier and more at ease in her manner when in the presence of others. Dress as well as your circumstances will permit and remember that it costs no more to dress becomingly than it does to don the wrong materials and colors.

Especial attention is given in this little work to the dressing of very stout, extremely short and unduly slender figures. All figures may be improved if we only know how to do it, and I trust in a practical manner to make this possible for my readers.

From my large correspondence, carried on in the *Ladies' Home Journal* upon this subject, I know that it is of general interest to an immense number of women who are obliged to do home dressmaking without any previous training.

It has not been found advisable to illustrate current fashions, as they change too quickly to become standard, but the main principles of cutting, fitting and finishing, like the brook, go on forever, and these once learned make even the race with Dame Fashion an easy one. Have patience, perseverance and care and you will accomplish wonders. Surely it is worth the trial if you only learn to gown yourself economically and becomingly. "Make haste slowly" in dressmaking.

Many terms used by dressmakers are of an unknown tongue to an amateur, so I have added a list of definitions that I hope will assist my readers over many a stumbling block and prove, like the rest of this work, "a friend in need."

Home Dressmaking.

❧ ❧ ❧

CHAPTER I.

THE NECESSARY IMPLEMENTS FOR SEWING.

NO WORKMAN can turn out good work without plenty of tools, and those of the right sort as well. When commencing home dressmaking keep in view this fact. Surely making a gown in a neat and becoming manner that will fit and then bear inspection is an art. This may be a real or acquired taste, but in either case it means to have perseverance, patience and a desire to excel for success to crown the effort. There are certain things that every workbasket must contain, and it should have a cover to keep out the dust. It is often a boon to home dressmakers to tell them what is the best brand or make of certain articles to use in their work. Unless placed so as to be able to try every new notion that comes out one cannot always know what is the best of its kind. For this reason I have given the names of several articles through this book, knowing them to be the foremost of their line and perfectly satisfactory in every respect. Many of them may be unfamiliar to my readers, but when tried they will soon prove indispensable to the workbasket and sewing-room.

The necessaries may be reckoned as a tracing wheel for marking patterns, a blue and black pencil for a similar use, plenty of Sovran pins of different sizes, an emery bag for needles that rust in perspiring hands and a bit of wax to draw silk through sometimes; the Cameo hooks and eyes, black and white, and automatic measure; belting tape in white, black or colors, cotton, silk or mixed; a strong linen tape measure and both flat and round bodkins for running in drawing strings, etc., are also among the "must haves." It will be found that a silver thimble costs very little nowadays, and if kept clean never stains the finger. Have large cutting shears and smaller scissors for general use, and keep them sharp. For ripping, keep either small pointed scissors or a penknife. Have an assortment of Milward's needles and use them for every material. Never hesitate to buy the best sewing silk and twist, for they will prove smooth, even, strong and fit for hand and machine sewing. That of M. Heminway & Sons is most favorably known in black and a large range of colors.

Use Clark's O. N. T. spool cotton, in white, fast black and colors, on any machine or in hand work. While sewing it is advisable to keep the hands smooth and' clean, as a gown soiled in the making is not worth finishing. For this use the purest of soaps—the Ivory—that is free from alkali. Patterns must be had, and the most Frenchy and original are those of the Morse-Broughton Company. A lapboard is a convenience, having one side hollowed out to fit into the form. In Chapter IX. there are full directions for sewing on the Omo dress shields, which should be considered among the indispensable articles of the workbasket. There are many shields for protecting the dress, but the only kind that is without rubber, odorless, impervious to perspiration, durable and very light in weight is the Omo.

A reliable sewing machine is the home dressmaker's best friend, who must, however, keep it well oiled and cleaned or it may prove cranky and contrary for the lack of proper attention. The Wheeler & Wilson No. 9 family sewing machine is light running, easy to handle, noiseless, speedy, and a saver of time, as well as a preserver of health for these very reasons. One cannot be too careful in selecting a machine, for upon its action depends the success of the work to be done, as well as the condition that the worker is left in. Follow the plain directions given and you cannot go astray with this machine, which is equally suitable for sewing every weight of material. Keep a stool for resting the feet when sewing, as such steady sitting in one position is tiresome. For the same reason—to be comfortable—cut on a low table, so that you can sit down to it. A dress form, the skirt part, is convenient for "hanging a skirt."

In the sewing-room there should be a closet for hanging partly made gowns and shelves or drawers for the store of necessary articles to be used in the art of dressmaking. Several boxes of good size are convenient for keeping old trimmings, goods to be sent to Lewando's dyehouse, ribbons, cotton, silk and woollen scraps and remnants of linings saved from other dressmaking sieges. The last finish to a dress is to fasten to the waist of it a sweet little sachet filled with J. & E. Atkinson's sachet powder, which is the most delicate way of perfuming a gown. Another plan is to keep similar sachets in the bureau drawers where dresses are laid, using violet, heliotrope, etc.

CHAPTER II.

CUTTING AND FITTING WAISTS.

THE first necessary article is a pattern, but do not expect a paper pattern—even one from the publishers of *L'Art de la Mode*—to fit you perfectly; it gives the general form of your waist, but must be fitted to *you*, not to an average figure, in order to set like a glove, smooth, without wrinkles, and with a pliable comfort, not a stiffness that prevents bending. Buy a paper

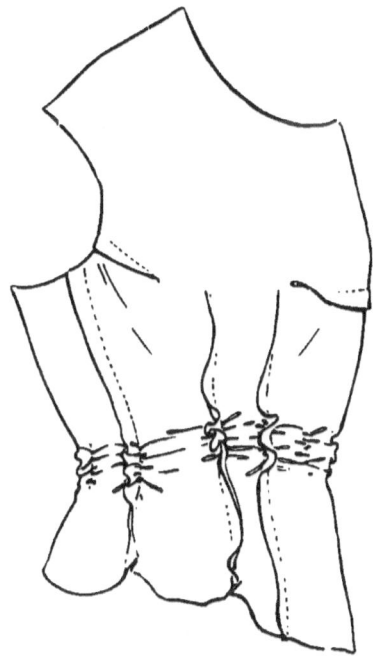

pattern of the Morse-Broughton Company, lay it on your lining, keeping the waistline exactly on the grain of the lining, which may be of silesia, sateen or percaline, in colors or in the "Nubian" fast black, but I prefer percaline — the soft finished — as it fits so well to the figure and is not heavy. As this black is thoroughly fast there need be no fear of its soiling the skin or underwear.

After pinning down the pattern use a tracing wheel, and allow, if it is not done on the pattern. half an inch for all seams, except the underarm and shoulders. where an inch is left. Do not cut out the darts until after trying on the lining, which should be cut two inches longer than the pattern, to allow for wrinkles that will probably be laid at the waistline. If you do not like the idea of these wrinkles, then do not allow any extra length for them. The first illustration shows a lining for a full-busted person, basted and the wrinkles laid in the lining, half an inch above, the same distance below and at the waistline, in order to take the strain from the outside material and to keep it smooth. The front edge is rounded over the bust and a small, crosswise dart taken halfway between the neck and waist. Another dart is taken in diagonally at the armhole, and this one is often used with advantage, even though the person is not full busted. These two darts appear only in the lining, the outside being smoothed over them.

Face the front edges of a waist that is rounded out with a piece of lining 1¼ inches wide cut the same shape as the edge. Do not cut off the front edges until after the fitting and pin them up on the figure by putting the selvedges together and the pins back. Commence at the waistline to pin, hook or button a dress and work up, smoothing all imperfections up toward the shoulders, as the French do. Sit down, stand up and bend over in a waist, as the fit may change with every position, and you want it to be right in each. In fitting shoulders do not take more off of the back than the front, unless the figure is very hollow in front. Baste all seams straight, and remember that as a basque is basted so it will be stitched, and upon this depends the beauty of the curving seams. Keep the waistline as long as it is naturally, not longer, and make the darts near together at waistline, to give them a slender look.

After having fitted the lining and pinned it for necessary alterations, using the Sovran pins, remove the bastings, mark where the stitching will be, cut out the two bust darts on each side and baste the lining to the outside. Put your first basting-thread exactly through the centre of the waistline, keeping the grain of each material straight. Now baste in the tiny wrinkles at the waistline, not putting them in plaits, but in wrinkles between each basting stitch. Do not cut the neck low in front, or the collar will not fit. Do not cut the armholes out in a lavish manner until the last thing, as they are apt to stretch. If thin around the neck place a layer of wadding—the sheet variety—between the lining and dress, tacking it here and there to the lining. If two layers of wadding are used the second one must be tapered down near the edges, and after stitching in the sleeves pull the wadding out of the seam, lest it be too clumsy. Small crescent-shaped pads are worn under the arms where every one is hollow. These are made of lining and wadding and reach a trifle more than halfway around the underpart of the arms, tapering to a point, and are tacked in lightly after the sleeves are sewed. It is well to sprinkle a little orris-root powder in these.

This illustration shows half of a flat paper pattern. As usually seen, the front edge is straight, but the artist has rounded it out a trifle, and in fitting it can be rounded more. There is the front piece containing two darts, the side gore, side form, and, finally, half of the back piece. This is for an ordinary figure and the last illustration of the series is for an extra large person— say 34-inch waist and 46-inch bust. This has an extra side gore, and prevents cutting any one piece so wide as to increase the size of the wearer. Seams decrease the width and add to the height, hence the necessity of this extra piece.

A new wrinkle in the preparation of a basque lining is to sew the finest haircloth on each side from the shoulder seam to the underarm seam, rounding it to fit in the armsize on the outer edge and allowing it to almost reach the collar on the inner side, then narrowing it down so that it is about nothing when it reaches the under seam. This takes in the hollow around the front of the arm and part of the collarbone, where the dress is very apt to wrinkle or "break," as it is styled by dressmakers, when the wearer moves. The haircloth is stiff enough to prevent this, and should be stitched on the lining between it and the outside fabric.

So exact has fitting become that basques of riding habits are interlined with this light, pliable haircloth in every part, to give the wearer the unwrinkled, erect appearance now desired. The perfect boning done with the featherbone and by the correct method will also make a better fit.

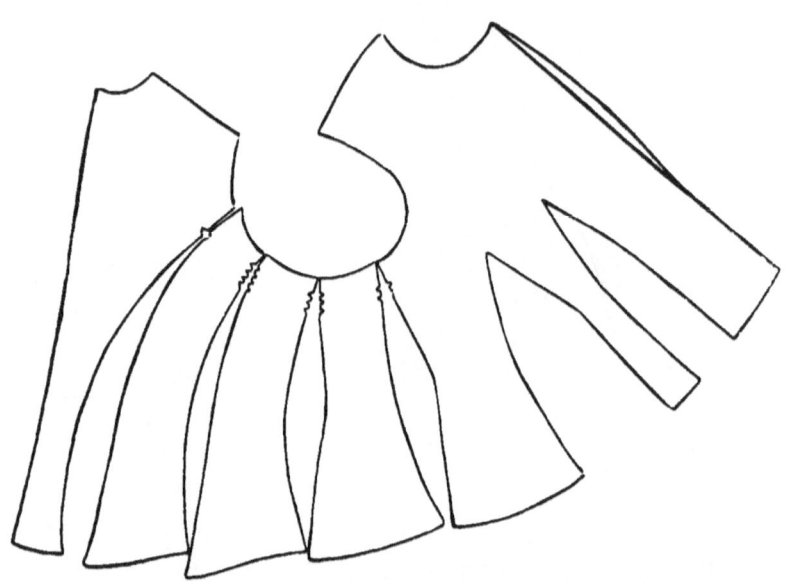

After the waist is fitted, with the outside basted on, the seams can be stitched barely outside of the basting, using M. Heminway & Sons' sewing silk for both strength and neatness, as the inside of the waist must look well and the seams must hold. Stitch on the machine with a tight tension and small stitch for waists and a long stitch for skirts. Overcast seams before pressing them (methods for this work are explained in the ninth chapter). Use a small, slender iron for pressing seams. Turn the side form, shoulder seams to the front, and open the darts, the back, side and underarm seams. Do not press plush, velvet or cloth seams, but stand the iron on a table and run the seams quickly over the rounded end. With a tailor-made suit the pressing is half the success of the gown; it is done with very heavy irons and by a man who nearly shapes the dress with his manipulations. It is said that tailors press or sponge cloths by laying a wet (not dripping) cloth on the right side of the goods and pressing it with a heavy hot iron until perfectly dry.

Do not cut into cloth without a thought of economy;

extravagant cutters are not the best dressmakers. The skirt portion of ripple basque pieces is interlined with very light haircloth and lined with silk as it shows here and there. High collars are cut with and without a seam at the back, the former fitting in closer to the neck. They are from 2 to 2½ inches high and interlined with light collar canvas. The outer material is turned over on the canvas and sewed down; the silk bias lining then basted on and hemmed down all around, sewing two Cameo hooks and eyes on the fronts so that the edges just meet. The dress neck is finished with a narrow bias binding of silk and the collar basted on the outside, holding the waist toward you. By the bye, in basting shoulder seams hold the back toward you, as that should be eased in a trifle. Press a collar on the wrong side. Fancy collars are described in the "Accessories of a Waist."

Sleeves are so various in style that it is useless to attempt describing the many fashions seen, but, if an amateur, get a flat paper pattern of the newest from *L'Art de la Mode*, and, if a professional dressmaker, invest at once in their made-up patterns, where you can see at a glance just how the sleeve, skirt, waist, etc., will look when made up. These fashions are all French, original, trustworthy and new. As a general rule to follow, remember to have a cross thread of your goods halfway between the elbow and shoulder, making the lower part bias and the inner seam on a straight line with the thumb when the arm is dropped by the side. Very thin arms were improved by a layer of wadding between the elbow and shoulders when close-fitting sleeves were worn. Cuffs and epaulette trimming shorten arms. A narrow tape may be stitched around the armholes with the sleeve, which prevents any splitting across the front of the basque. The armholes are closely but loosely overcast; the sleeve seams are clipped several times to prevent any drawing, overcast separately and pressed open if desired. Tapes with which to hang the basque are sewed on in a loop at the joining of the side-form seams and armsizes.

The wrist of the sleeve should be faced with a bias piece of silk the color of the dress or its trimmings and the inner seam left open for an inch to allow the band to pass through. The sleeves must be pinned on the wearer, as some need the underarm seam nearer the front than others. Too tight a sleeve over the forearm makes the hands red. Never show the wristbone unless you have pretty hands, as shortened sleeves make them very conspicuous. Just at present the fashion is for full soft sleeves, but they need a trifle bolstering up for all that. This is given by two box-plaited ruffles of fine haircloth, hemmed, lapped over each other and sewed to the upper part of the lining sleeve just below the elbow, this being the only interlining for a large puff. A small puff or drapery at the top of the sleeve needs only one ruffle. These ruffles do not extend under the arm. At the present time sleeves are cut very long, some forming a point over the back of the hand in Renaissance style.

The fitting and making of cotton goods that will some day seek the seclusion of a washtub differ in many respects from the method of fashioning the silk and woollen materials described. I do not advise making up plaid ginghams on the bias, as they are apt to be pulled askew in the ironing.

Waists and sleeves of such fabrics are made with the bag or French seams, which have the raw edges put together on the right side and a very narrow seam taken; then they are turned to the wrong or inner side and another tiny seam taken. Wash waists are best lined with a piece of the same goods or with white lawn. If one perspires freely there should be a deep yoke at least of the goods on the wrong side; with others a reënforcement around the armholes and down the side seams is sufficient. The round waists worn under the skirt should extend fully three inches below the waistline. They are usually finished around the waist with a narrow casing or strip of the goods through which runs white elastic a fourth of an inch wide and an inch smaller than the belt measure. This keeps the waist down, and the wearer can move the fullness to the centre, back and front, when the waist is on. Pearl buttons and hand-worked button-holes fasten the fronts.

Embroidery is the usual trimming in edging or insertings. In buying such trimmings remember that the patterns having small holes wear the best. Have cotton gowns washed out quickly and dried in the shade, for while the reliable brands of goods are fast in color, it is simply tempting them to fade if they are hung in a July sun. As a precaution, use good—not strong—soap and the shady side of the yard. Stitch the seams of wash goods with Clark's O. N. T. spool thread, which is satisfactory for hand or machine sewing. In place of making up cotton shirt waists buy the ready-made Griffon brand.

CHAPTER III.

THE BINDING OF A SKIRT.

ONE of the most important features of a well-finished skirt is the binding of the lower edge. It must be both useful and ornamental, thoroughly protect the edge of the dress goods and afford a neat finish at the same time. It has been found that a good quality of bias velveteen is the best binding for many reasons. Velveteen is sufficiently soft not to rub the shoes shabby, yet closely woven so as to resist wear. The S. H. & M. bias velveteen bindings are cut a perfectly true bias, and will, therefore, fit smoothly around the edge of any skirt, no matter how it may be shaped. This brand of binding always has S. H. & M. on the label, and from now on the binding will also be stamped with the three magic letters on the back of every yard or two of the material. The Duxbak rainproof binding is recommended for storm dresses, as it has a finish that sheds water.

The easiest method of binding with one of these pieces of bias velveteen is as follows: Lay the right side of the binding next to the right side of the goods and baste smoothly on, allowing a full inch of the dress goods and lining to turn up and a fourth of an inch of the binding. Stitch on the machine and turn the binding and dress goods over on the wrong side. Baste the velveteen down near the edge, allowing the merest trifle of the folded edge to project evenly below the skirt itself. Then turn and baste the raw edge of the binding down and hem it so that none of the stitches will show on the right side. Pull out the bastings, lay a piece of crinoline over the velveteen and press it with a warm iron.

Thus the binding will really protect the dress by taking the wear and tear first. The velveteen should exactly match the color of the dress goods, which is easily done, as it can be found in several hundred shades, and affords a dainty finish to the garment. The basting and pressing are very important parts of this work. In basting hold the binding toward you. Do not cut the edge of a skirt of the proper length, but allow it to be fully an inch too long, and turn this portion up over on wrong side with the velveteen binding. As these bindings are made of double-warp yarns they are very durable, and from the fact of the close pile surface all dust and mud are easily brushed off.

The tailor's favorite manner of binding is to fold the bias velveteen binding in the middle and lay it against the right side of the skirt, with the raw edges even and the lining—not the interlining—left separate. After basting together stitch and turn the edges up, leaving the folded edge of velveteen to project nearly a fourth of an inch below the skirt. The lining is then basted down over the raw edges, hemmed, and a warm iron applied over a piece of thin crinoline, which saves the goods from any accidental scorching. While this manner of binding has many advocates, I must confess a preference for the first style described, in which the velveteen also answers for a narrow facing. It can readily be seen that in order to have a binding perfectly smooth it must be cut a true bias, so as to adapt itself to a gored, circular, fluted or plain skirt.

The bias velveteen with a cord edge of this brand that is just making its bow to the vast army of home dressmakers has the upper edge turned and stitched down ready to blindstitch on, and thus saves time for the busy woman and leaves a pretty, even, round cord on the skirt edge that will not rub out, owing to its filling. This cord takes the place of the piping so dearly loved by tailors as a finish to their costumes for ladies. Silk, alpaca, moreen, etc., petticoats should also have a velveteen binding, to save the edge from cutting out. Although seemingly a small item of the skirt, the binding is one of the parts that cannot be omitted. It adds to the length of service and gives a better appearance to the skirt, in view of which, my dear sisters of the needle, is it not worth putting on the binding correctly and using the right kind of one? The cord edge is called the Ever-Ready.

The Velveteen Featherbone Binding has a row of featherboning stitched on one edge, which is placed against the lower edge of the right side of the skirt and a row of stitching run half-way between the edge and the stitches already there. This holds the bone firmly to the skirt, and even should the bias velveteen wear out the featherboning will remain in place. Then turn up the skirt and blindstitch down the upper edge of the binding, which is already turned and hemmed to save time and basting. Some dressmakers featherstitch the raw edge of a binding down, but it takes longer and requires much nicer work than to hem it down with blind stitches that must not go through to the right side.

The Redfern binding, which is one of the same brand, is a corded velvet that has a very handsome appearance when applied in either of the styles described above. Velveteen bindings may be had in widths from 1¼ to 2 inches, and in lengths suitable for all skirts.

CHAPTER IV.

THE USE OF VELVET.

IN making up velvet waists, capes, skirts, etc., some new rules have to be followed that will not apply to other fabrics. It is a material that is becoming to all complexions and ages and exercises a softening effect upon all defects. As a trimming it enriches silk, woollen and cotton goods with which it may be combined, and as a costume it surpasses in beauty, style and richness any other fabric.

Velvet is never out of fashion, therefore it can never prove an unwise purchase. An all-silk velvet, like black pearls, is beyond the purse of any but a few of fortune's favorites, but in the "Boulevard" velvet my interested readers will find a fabric like silk velvet in appearance and feel, surpassing it in wear and costing about one-fourth its price. The close, thick pile enables one to use it cut on the straight or bias, and as it is made in black and all staple and fashionable shades there is no lack of variety in its colorings for any purpose.

Velvet garments must have each piece cut the same way of the goods or the different parts will take on many shadings; the pile must run downward. Keep your wits about you when cutting out a velvet garment, and in basting it use a fine needle and silk, as coarse cotton leaves an impression on the soft velvet pile or surface. When ripping out basting threads cut them every inch, so as to have only a short piece to pull through. Use the small, smooth black pins for fitting, and do not allow yourself the habit that even professional dressmakers sometimes have of putting in pins and taking them out, apparently at haphazard. Let each pin go into the waist, etc., with a purpose, and do not use any more than are absolutely necessary in velvet. Carefully stitch the seams, for one altered means a line in any velvet, even the thick-piled "Boulevard," which, by the way, is stamped on the back of every yard, so you can see for yourself if you receive what is asked for.

If any part of the velvet becomes creased, then steam it according to the directions given in the chapter on "Renovating Materials." To press the seams of a velvet garment stand a warm—not hot—iron on the back end and run the open or closed seams over the small, round end, after the slightest dampening possible of each seam. This prevents flattening the pile, as ironing would do.

When a dress is trimmed with velvet always have it near the face. A velvet collarette, sleeves or plastron is very becoming for a too-slender form. Velvet skirts can be worn with chiffon, silk or velvet waists. A black velvet cape is a joy forever with any gown suitable for street or evening wear. Girls from three years of age wear velvet trimmings and small boys have velvet jacket suits, so it is really for all ages.

In hemming a bias piece of velvet turn the hem down but once and blindstitch it along with stitches that catch on the under side only, never showing on the right side, from a half to an inch apart. Never work a buttonhole in velvet. When dusty, wipe velvet with an old silk handkerchief or brush with a soft whisk, called a velvet broom. The material wears well, but give it care and it will do better than well.

At present velvet is in the height of style for blouses or fancy waists for cool Spring days, and for trimmings and capes. Even during midsummer velvet crush collars, belts and knots will be worn, and the indications for Fall point to this fabric being more in vogue than ever. During the Fall and Winter entire costumes, capes, coats, single skirts and odd waists, trimmings and different accessories for silk and woollen gowns of the ever-becoming velvet will flourish like a green bay tree.

CHAPTER V.

CUTTING AND FITTING SKIRTS.

IN CHAPTERS III. and VIII. the correct manner of binding and interlining skirts is given fully. More attention should be paid to linings in general, and especially linings for skirts. Silk is beyond the reach of three-fourths of the feminine population, but this need not discourage one, for the "Nubian" fast-black percaline will supply its place at a small cost. Make a note of the name being stamped on the selvedge in red letters, for there are many so-called "fast blacks," but only one "Nubian." The percaline has a high finish, like silk, a stiffness reminding one of taffeta, and moiré markings that make it a handsome lining as well as a durable and reliable one that will never stain or crock the underwear. This dye is applied to percalines, sateens, silesias, cambrics, etc.

As four-fifths of the dress skirts made should be lined with black it is well to know of the best. If a still cheaper lining is wished try the paper cambric, but always take the stiffened while the present style of skirts last. Nothing soft or clinging is wanted for a really stylish skirt. Silesia is sometimes used for skirts, but moiréd percaline is the first choice, and it comes in several grades. Besides selecting a handsome and durable lining get a good skirt pattern, such as is issued by the Morse-Broughton Company, which will be carefully shaped and notched so that the veriest amateur may put it together. The average skirt this season is 5½ yards wide and 41 inches long, requiring six yards of percaline to line it.

Take four measures for a skirt, centre front, back and each side, as the hips are not always the same height. Cut the lining out first, baste the interlining of haircloth to it, as described in a following chapter, and then baste in the dress goods. Use Milward's needles and medium thread—O. N. T. No. 40—for basting. Pin the seams together before basting them and commence at the top to baste, holding the bias or gored edge toward you. The newest skirts are fitted without darts in front and a very stout figure will require a few gathers there, but the narrow top fits itself easily to an ordinary figure. The lining and dress goods must be exactly alike, and both cut with a cross thread perfectly straight. When this is done there is no trouble in making up the lining and outside separate, which many report "will not hang together." When haircloth is put on properly, viz., laid and lapped over the lining seams, the lining and material cannot be sewed together in the seams lower than the top of the interlining. Then each is stitched, the haircloth applied and the two finished seams caught together.

In this case the seams would be cut evenly and overcast or bound with a bias strip of the lining, after pressing them open, and then binding all raw edges together. The handsomest skirts have lining and outside made separate, seams pressed and then overcast, interlining sewed to the lining and the two caught together down each seam; or the outside is seamed up, the interlining basted to it and each piece of lining basted down the seams, one edge even, the other and the upper one turned down and blindstitched neatly. Then the lower edge of the dress goods is turned under and the lining blindstitched to it. The bias velveteen binding is then sewed on by hand, not turning any of the skirt up with it, but sewing the right side of the binding to the lining, turning it up, leaving a roll like a piping to protect the dress edge, and hemming down the upper edge, after basting it.

The easiest way of lining a skirt is to baste the interlining to the lining, letting each edge come out evenly, then baste to the outside material; stitch, press the seams, bind with a strip of lining, after cutting the haircloth nearly out of the seams, and overcast the raw lower edge before putting on the bias velveteen binding. Although easy for an amateur, the skirt will not set as well as if the haircloth—I mean pure haircloth and not the cotton haircloth—was applied as described in Chapter VIII. If your skirt pattern directs that an elastic, a quarter of an inch wide, be run across the rounded or godet plaits, to hold them in position, put it on; otherwise omit it, as all skirts do not need it. Be very careful about shaping your skirt around the lower edge.

If a belt is used have the outside of the dress material cut bias and lined with the skirt lining cut straight. Put a stitch of white thread at the centre front of the belt. Hold the skirt toward you when basting it to the lining, then cover the raw edge with the material, stitched down. Do not try to get a "skin-tight" fit over the hips and "ease" the front in the belt as you baste it. Lay the centre back in single or double box plaits or simply gather it, as your *L'Art de la Mode* pattern may direct. Allow a lap of half an inch on each side of the belt for the Cameo hook and eye and sew them near the lower edge of the belt. A favorite way of finishing the top of a skirt for a stout or short-waisted person is to simply pipe or cord the edge with a piece of the goods, which allows it to fall lower on the waistline. The French do not like belts, and their modistes know more little quirks of this kind than we do.

A safety hook and eye can be sewed halfway down the opening or placket hole, which should be fully 10 inches long, faced narrowly, turned in an inch on each side and gathered or plaited in with the lining and outside, which prevents any gaping. Sew two sets of Clinton skirt supporters to your skirt, the ones with the hook to the skirt and those with an eye to the waist, and remove all danger of the two garments separating. Sew the pocket in the right back seam, the top of the opening being four or five inches below the top of the skirt. Always face the inside of the pocket with the dress goods and leave the opening large enough to get the hand in without straining the stitches. Allow a quarter of an inch at the top of a skirt for the belt or piping and half an inch at the lower edge for turning up. A street skirt should hang evenly all around and not touch the ground. Put a loop of tape on each side, near the back, to hang the skirt up by.

A well-fitting petticoat adds much to the success of a skirt, and if a silk one cannot be afforded excellent ones can be made of the finer grades of "Nubian" percaline, having the soft rustle and lightness of silk. Make it on a yoke; have it three yards wide, faced, and then bind with the bias velveteen featherbone binding, which will keep the petticoat comfortably extended; add three bias gathered ruffles, overlapping each other, each five inches wide and the top one with an erect heading; finish the top with a yoke four inches deep; no opening, but a drawstring in the back from the side seams where the yoke ends, the back being faced. A skirt of wash goods is cut nowadays with the same gored seams on the front and sides as any other, with a few gathers at the top and the mass of fullness gathered to the centre back. The seams should be basted, stitched, pressed and then each raw edge turned in and overcast. A five to seven inch hem finishes the edge. Where a lining is necessary, as with an organdie, have it of silk or lawn, made up separate and finished with a ruffle or only a hem; this should be certainly four yards wide, with an organdie five yards. Have plenty of it and do it correctly. A tiny cushion, of curled hair and the lining, is generally put in the centre back of a skirt, where nearly every one is hollow, but it must not show, only round out the figure indistinctly. A skirt of many gores adds to the apparent height.

CHAPTER VI.

BONING A WAIST WITH FEATHERBONE.

NEXT in importance to the fitting of a waist comes the boning, and upon the atter much of the fitting depends. If well boned and the right spring given to each bone the waist will not have a wrinkle in it, and the easiest process of boning is that done with Featherbone, which is unlike all other boning in process and effect. It is only recently that dressmakers have learned how to use this bone so as to obtain the best results, and the manufacturers have increased the styles of and uses for Featherbone until it seems impossible to make up a dress properly without using it.

In the first place have the attachment that will fit any sewing machine for holding the Featherbone in position. Commence to bone at the seam left of front and have the under left of seam on top. The first thing to do is to put the wrong side of the Featherbone up under the machine so that the needle will be exactly in the middle of it. Then place the attachment on, with groove over the bone, and fasten it firmly with the thumbscrew. Commence at the top of the seam and stitch downward, following closely to line of seam-stitching but not over it, with left side of seam up. For the first few inches crowd the goods under the needle a little, then stitch smoothly along to within an inch of the waistline. Here you can obtain a spring by raising the short waist and bone toward the back of the machine foot and against it. You can regulate the spring by the manner in which this is raised. As soon as the Featherbone is secured in the attachment cut it off the right length and give no further heed to it, for the attachment keeps it straight.

If boning a long basque continue from two inches below the waistline to the end by crowding or easing the seam toward the needle, making the bone tighter than the seam and thereby securing a handsome curve over the hip and preventing all rolling up. Finish off the end of the bone by first tying the threads, then rip the covering for half an inch, then cut off the stay, thinning and rounding the corners, and turn over the end of the cover, not drawing it too tightly; secure with a few stitches and, finally, bend the top of the bone back a trifle and you have a firmly boned seam, shaped to a perfect contour from being caught all along the seam in place of only here and there, as all other boning is done. Use silk on the machine. Of course, the seams are all pressed and overcast before boning. Bone the seams to top of corset, except the second seam from centre back, which is boned to the armsize to prevent any break in the bodice.

These waist bones are in lengths of 12 yards and are of every color, covered with satin, silk, moiré, Prussian and twill. The hook and eye bone is used only for the front edges, and prevents gaping, breaking or wrinkling; is sewed firmly to the edge and is stiffer than the waist bone. For an evening waist the eyelet bone—narrower than these mentioned—should be used and the eyelets for the lacing cord worked on the inner side. It has been the custom to put canvas around the edge of the basque to hold it in shape, but among the various styles of Featherbone is one known as soft bone, which is stitched to the bottom of the waist, then turned up and caught firmly to the ends of the stay bones. If a waist opens on the shoulder seam and along one side put a soft bone down the shoulders to keep the hooked edge firm and even.

The Featherbone tape comes in four widths, one-half to two inches, and is suitable for the lower edge of basques also, especially if of heavy goods. The tapes are also used for godet rings, that are sewed inside of the three godet flutes at the back of a silk, alpaca, sateen, etc., petticoat, three smaller ones about five inches below the waistline and three larger 10 inches above the lower edge, inside of each flute. Such a petticoat then has a ruffle around the lower edge with skirt bone run in the hem and at the shirred top, in place of a cording, and the ruffle is tacked down in even flutes all around, making a perfect support for the dress skirt to hang over. Another plan is to omit the skirt bone in the ruffle and place it at the lower edge of the skirt. This will set better if sewed through firmly to the wrong side of the petticoat, then turned up, leaving the bone like a cord. If a very flaring effect is wished on a petticoat the Duplex skirt bone or Featherbone tapes may be used.

Sleeves are enlarged with a layer of tarlatan having three rounded rows of the Duplex skirt bone and one upright support of the same kind, which holds out any sleeve except the puffed. The latter needs a straight piece of tarlatan having several upright rows of Duplex skirt bone with the upper and lower edges gathered together, making a soft puff. The former come ready-made. This same bone is used in high flaring collars on jackets and capes and will always retain its shape. The very lightest weight of interlining is recommended for collars, revers and cuffs when using Featherbone. The five-cord tape is used for ordinary collars, cuffs and revers, and skirt bone is also used on revers, the beauty of which rests in their never having turnover points, which the Featherbone effectually prevents. Lovely piping or cording for dress trimming is made with a small Featherbone cord, which has a perfect effect. It appears that one might go on forever finding new uses for the varieties of Featherbone, for the story is not yet half told.

And now the question arises, "What is Featherbone?" It is made of the pointer quill of the turkey, which is split, finely shredded and bound into cords, forming an unbreakable bone; also one that is elastic, light and never injured by perspiration. It adapts itself to any curve, hence its success as a waist bone. It possesses a certain stiffness, yet is pliable. It is made up wide and narrow, heavy and medium weight and extra thin, and is not affected by the temperature or wear. It will not break in actual use, and is as suitable for a stout as for a thin figure— even more so, as it shapes even a poor figure when the waist is properly boned. Even milliners have seen the practical use of Featherbone and are using the soft bone in bows to support the loops. It is one of the really good aids to home dressmaking that have been invented. It is simple to use, quickly manipulated, inexpensive in cost, and adds much to the beauty of a well-fitting waist, which also means a well-boned waist.

CHAPTER VII.

ACCESSORIES OF A WAIST.

EVEN after a waist is cut, fitted and stitched there are many extra pieces or accessories that rightfully belong to it, and these make the waist plain or elaborate, according to their form and material. Among these extras are cuffs, collarettes, vests, plastrons, belts, revers, fancy collars and basque pieces. Velvet, silk, satin, lace, chiffon or contrasting woollen goods are the usual materials selected for such articles. They must either perfectly match the foundation color of the dress itself or offer a harmonizing contrast to it.

Cuffs are just reappearing, after being somewhat neglected for several seasons, but they are different to the old turnover cuff. Now they are nearly circular, being eight inches wide around the hand, two and a half inches deep and fourteen inches wide at the top. They are interlined with fine haircloth, turning each edge over, and lined with the dress goods or silk, as they flare sufficiently to show the lining. The cuff may be left partly open in a tiny V at the inside sleeve seam or made large enough to slip over the hand with this seam—it's only one—closed, though there may be a V in the sleeve beneath. The top and bottom edges of the outside material are turned over on the inner side and caught down; then the lining, which is cut in the same shape, is hemmed on, an eighth of an inch below each edge. The cuff is then slipstitched to the edge of the sleeve, which is already faced.

In pressing facings rip out the basting threads first and use a piece of thin crinoline between the facing and iron, in order to prevent any discoloration. Cuffs shorten the apparent length of the arms. Other trimmings on the sleeve edge are a twist of ribbon, velvet, etc., with a bow at the back, a band of lace insertion or passementerie. Another style shows trimmings of any of these materials put on in three diagonal rows, each ending

31

with a knot of the same toward the back and nearly to the elbow, the other end commencing at the inner seam. A large scroll figure of braiding is used on the top of the wrist. A frill of lace, using it always three times as full as the space to which it is gathered, finishes many home and dressy costumes and imparts a delicate appearance to the hands. It is not out of place, however, to leave the lower edge of any sleeve untrimmed.

Revers are a boon to hollow-chested persons, as they fill up the space, and they are also becoming to full-busted women, as they detract from any oversize if pointed long and slender below the fullest part. They are of the dress goods or a contrasting material, and are finished with an edge of beading, braided, stitched in two rows on the machine, a delicate vine of lace appliquéd on, etc. Revers are now made in so many shapes—square, pointed, continue over the shoulders to form epaulettes, etc.—that it is impossible to describe them all, but their making follows the same general lines.

They are interlined with crinoline or haircloth, depending upon the outside material needing a firm or very thin stiffening. The outside material must be turned over the stiffening, caught down with a few long stitches and the silk or dress goods lining hemmed over this, an eighth of an inch from the edge. Cut all such accessories out of paper first and pin them on before a looking glass until the proper position is found. Some revers are cut in one piece with the jacket fronts. When very wide they are styled Directoire. If they taper to a point at the waistline the wearer will appear longer waisted. If they start from the shoulder seam and taper to the waistline they are properly termed bretelles.

Shawl revers have a rolled collar below a standing one that ends in short, wide revers over the bust without the notch or "step" that distinguishes a man's coat collar. This latter style has the revers part joined to the turnover collar, which is sewed to the dress neck with the seam toward the inside, leaving the dress goods free to be hemmed down over the seam. The revers are seamed in at the end of the collar and sewed in the front edge of the jacket, with the same seaming or made entirely separate, finished up and then slightly lapped over the collar ends. Revers are always in fashion, but their shape may differ very much. At present the short, wide ones are stylish, with the outer point very loosely caught down or left free.

Basques or pieces to represent the skirt of a bodice are added to a round waist, fitted to the bottom of the waistline, and to slightly pointed ones as well. They are usually in flutes or ripples, are cut nearly circular and are from four to six inches deep when finished. The upper part is sewed on plainly, being seamed to the waist edge, with the lining hemmed down over it, leaving the lower edge to form flutes or godets on the sides and across the back. The front is plain or the basque piece may commence only at the hips or second dart. The piece must be interlined with haircloth and prettily lined, as the under part shows. Sometimes the flutes have a tiny ribbon run around half way up, to keep them tacked in position.

The lower edge is stitched or left plain or cut in square tabs, and each one braided. The upper edge is often concealed by a band of passementerie, a twist of ribbon ending in a bow on one side, a bias band of the dress goods braided or a fold of velvet or silk, which is sewn down all around and a three-inch point left beyond the centre front, which is lapped over and hooked under a couple of pointed ends. Even on a round waist point this belt slightly at the centre, back and front, to give a long-waisted effect.

There is a crush belt that gives a similar appearance, being fitted to the lower part of the waistline, like a short yoke, and boned three times in front, twice at the back and once on each side. The lining is flat and the bias outside material is laid in soft folds over it, being turned over an inch on the stiff interlining upon which the lining is hemmed down. A bow at the back finishes the article, which is two inches wide there and three inches in front. The Empire belt is fitted around and above the waist, is three to seven inches wide, and in soft folds or flat. If the latter, it is covered with embroidery or beading; in either case it is lined, interlined and boned, and is only suitable for a slender figure.

A two-inch ribbon or belting belt is becoming to nearly any figure. Even No. 9 —1½ inches—is fashionable this season. A slender, narrow buckle makes the waist smaller. There are many contrivances for holding skirts and waists together under a belt. Nothing can look more untidy than a gap between a belt and skirt. Keep your belt well pushed down in front, as it is one of the first signs of middle age for a belt to ride up at that part. The lighter colored the belt the larger the waist.

The regular crush belts are rather *passé*, but they were always bias, fastened with the two frilled ends at the back, were hemmed at each side and cut twice as wide as they would be when finished. The narrow, folded belt now worn is of bias velvet or silk or of five-inch ribbon, and is folded once or twice around the waist; it hooks at the back under a short, flat bow of two ends and loops or four pointed ends and a knot.

Fancy collars rank among the very important parts of a waist nowadays. The manner of making the ordinary collar is explained in the chapter on cutting and fitting a waist. The usual crush collar, also called a stock, is made of a perfectly bias piece of silk or velvet nine inches wide and an inch longer than the collar is to be. This is laid over a piece of cross-barred crinoline, shaped to fit the neck and opening in the back. The illustrations show such an interlining shaped to open at the back and one to open in front, as the false collar sewed to the dress neck would do that affords a support to the fancy collar. The designs differ in shape, and the only way to get a perfect fit is to experiment with paper until it is found.

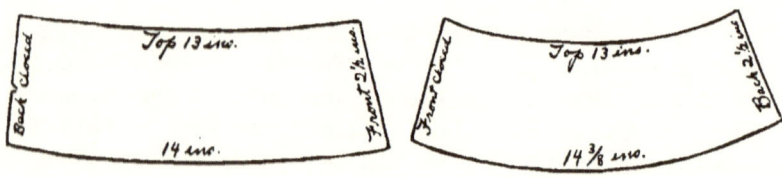

The bias material is turned over on the wrong side of the interlining and hemmed down with a raw edge. Then arrange the rest of the goods in easy folds, catching them here and there. Now cover the wrong side with a piece of bias silk and hem it down; fasten with two hooks and eyes at the ends. If a frill is wanted at the back leave ends 1½ inches longer, double them over and shirr; then fasten, leaving two frills standing out. Nowadays a bow of two wide loops and two short ends is preferred to the frills, but the latter are more becoming to a full face.

Ribbon collars are of five-inch ribbon, folded once around the neck and tied in the short, wide bow at the back. This often fits without any shaping, but some necks require a little dart or V taken in at the centre front. A pretty finish to one of these collars is a ruffle of 2½-inch lace, using a yard, turned over the top, to fall as it will. Then there are points and tabs trimmed with lace or beading and turned over, and the nearly circular collar piece similar to the circular cuff; but these are merely passing fancies and would not be useful if illustrated in a standard work.

The large collarettes and epaulettes or sleeve caps worn are interlined with crinoline or haircloth, according to the material, and lined with silk or the dress goods. These, too, change so often that it is impossible to describe them. Study your figure before adopting such an accessory. It was designed to fill in hollow shoulders and to widen sloping figures; if not of such a figure you do not need this style, which conceals defects, but does not heighten natural charms. All accessories tend to make a gown more dressy and more becoming if rightly selected, but try the effect in paper on the wearer before cutting into the goods.

Flat vests may be pointed, rounded just to reach the waist-line or cut in a regular waistcoat shape below the waistline, separating at the waist. They are fitted with one or two darts, as the fullness of the figure may require, when worn under a jacket basque, as then they are sewed in at the side seams with the outside material or form a separate garment, with a back of lining fastening up the centre and shaped like two back and side gore pieces.

Other vests are merely applied to the centre of the waist in a certain shape, long and narrow, etc. Others are sewed down on one side, the right, and lapped over on the left, fastening with hooks and worked eyelets over the dress or under a bretelle or revers trimming, with the regular waist hooking up in the centre beneath the vest. A short square or V-shaped waist gives the wearer a fuller figure, while one slender and pointed at the waistline adds to the length of the waist.

A vest is usually in contrast, as it is intended for a trimming as well as often an addition to eke out a made-over gown. Velvet, plain and figured silk, cloth, etc., are the materials usually selected. Plain cloth or serge covered with a braiding of black or gilt soutache braid makes a handsome vest. The pieces are cut out and then stamped with an allover scroll pattern, upon which the braid is sewn with silk, then pressed on the wrong side, and the vest is finally made up. Double-breasted vests fastening with two rows of buttons and having a small turnover collar like that on a man's vest are worn with a linen chemisette to fill up the V space above. A vest must serve a purpose, either as a trimming or part of the gown, or its force is lost.

A plastron might be defined as a loose vest, as it answers the same purpose, and is made of the same materials as well as of

35

thin fabrics like chiffon and nets that will look well in a loose, fluffy mass. This accessory is not only becoming to a tall and slender figure, but on a stout form conceals the waistline if dropped low in front, and that point is the telltale on a full figure.

Plastrons to wear with a jacket are made entirely separate from a waist, with a crush collar and a lining back, as described for vests. They are also attached to the dress on one side and hooked over on the other, gathering the fullness at the top in a wide or narrow space, as is the most becoming. The lower edge is gathered, turned up underneath and allowed to drop slightly or much, as the figure may require. When made of a transparent material a plastron must be lined with silk.

In using chiffon for such a purpose remember how gauzy it is and gather the full width, 40 inches, into a narrow plastron. A width of silk—20 inches—is used for this, or a half-width of woollen goods 40 inches wide. Velvet makes a handsome plastron to wear with a jacket waist. With such a one the fronts from the centre fullness to the side seams must be faced with the material in the plastron, as it may sometimes show under the opened fronts.

CHAPTER VIII.

THE PROPER USE OF HAIRCLOTH.

ABUSE a friend and you can hardly expect him to give you his best efforts, and yet this is what half the professional and amateur dressmakers do with haircloth. They do not understand using it, and thus do not obtain the best results, for which haircloth is blamed. Rid yourself of the idea that any substitute will have the same effect as haircloth.

The latter is made of genuine horsehair—that is, what is manufactured by the American Hair Cloth Company is—which will keep in place when crushed in packing or sitting and will, like truth, always rise again. Horsehair woven into haircloth keeps its elastic and resilient qualities and may bend for a time, but never break. It is light in weight, comes in black, gray and white, and forms a perfect interlining for skirts, sleeves, revers, basque backs, riding habits, etc. It must be cut crosswise—remember that in the beginning—and also take heed of the fact that there are cotton imitations of haircloth which I do not recommend, as I believe in using an interlining that will have the flaring effect at all times, in damp and dry weather and under all circumstances.

In using haircloth to interline a skirt have it from 10 to 20 inches deep; if it is a trained skirt interline it the depth of the train and 20 inches above the ground as well. First have the lining seamed up, then lay the haircloth on the wrong side of it and lap each width over the other, cutting it crosswise. Bind each edge of the lapped part with a bias strip of the lining and stitch together; then stitch the upper edge to the lining, leaving the lower part basted only.

Put the dress skirt, which has the seams stitched, to the lining so that the raw edges of both come together and arrange the seams as described in the chapter devoted to the cutting of

37

skirts. As all skirts should be left at first fully an inch too long, then turn up the lower edge to the proper wearing length and continue the binding as explained in the chapter on binding skirts, but never cut the haircloth off at the bottom edge too short to turn it up. Such a skirt sets with a graceful flare and stands out from the wearer, aiding her to walk in a free, unencumbered manner. It is also light in weight, which both health and comfort depend upon.

Riding-habit bodices are interlined through the postillion or skirt part of the back, across the shoulders and chest, to give them the most exact fit without a wrinkle. All basques having a fluted or godet or box-plaited back need this interlining to keep them in shape. For the same reason we apply an interlining to cuffs, the various revers now in style and the large collarettes of many shapes. Large collars on capes, revers on jackets and the skirt back of the latter garment are treated in the same way. Although sufficiently stiff to keep its shape, haircloth can be sewed on the machine without any trouble.

For sleeves it is better to use the haircloth in three box-plaited ruffles placed on the top half of the sleeve lining, reaching from just below the shoulder nearly to the elbow. This gives the puff, bishop and leg-of-mutton sleeves a soft, drooping appearance, without allowing them to hang perfectly flat. This method of interlining is explained at length in the chapter on fitting waists.

The inexperienced dressmaker who finds it difficult to make her lining skirt separate from the dress fabric can lay the haircloth between the lining and goods and stitch it in the seams, then bind the seams with a bias strip of the lining; but I will warn her in advance that while this will look better than any other facing or interlining, it will not have the same flare as it does when each piece is lapped over, as previously described.

Some ladies wear a petticoat of haircloth made with a yoke and upper part of sateen, for the sake of its lightness; then a Spanish flounce (18 inches deep) of haircloth is box plaited on the front and sides and godet flutes used at the back. This flounce is turned up at the lower edge, faced with sateen and finished with a bias velveteen binding or braid, making a skirt for all gowns, though personally I prefer a silk petticoat and interlined dress skirt. Haircloth has a niche of its own, and is one of those fortunate or unfortunate articles used in dressmaking that cannot have a satisfactory substitute.

CHAPTER IX.

THE FINISHINGS OF A WAIST.

NEXT to the boning of a waist comes the hooks and eyes in importance, both as to the kind used and the manner of sewing them on. A hook should not be too large, should have a long, slender bill, with a safety spring at the under part to keep it fastened. The Cameo hooks and eyes will be found perfectly capable of answering the above description; they are also gotten up in a unique manner, every card bearing the name Cameo, with the hooks and eyes set on crosswise and a patent automatic sewing measure attached lengthwise to every card. This measure is one of the most convenient little affairs, divided from eighths to full inches, and is for measuring the distance between hooks and eyes, buttons and buttonholes, and for a guide in turning up a hem, folding tucks, etc. The hooks and eyes on the front edges of a bodice should be half an inch apart, the hooks on the right side. The properly made bodice has a featherbone stay up each front edge to the height of the darts.

On the left under side of this place the eyes, so that they barely project beyond the edge. Sew with five stitches in each loop and four on the right side of the large part of the eye, halfway to the top, and then pass on to the next one, without breaking the Heminway silk or twist, after measuring the distance with the little automatic measure. For a neat finish cover the eyes with an inch facing of silk, cut bias and blindstitched, the turned edge coming nearly to the top of the eye, the latter being left free to catch the hook easily. On the right side the hooks are put back a trifle from the edge, so that when hooks and eyes are attached the edges will meet. The hooks are sewed with five stitches in each small loop, taking them straight back, and at the extreme top of the bill five more stitches are taken crosswise, without interfering with the safety spring in the slightest. When the facing is put on the hook side it must not come over the spring—only to the lower part of it. If covered it will not have the same freedom of action. Many dressmakers err in this respect and then censure the maker of the hooks. Do not cover the spring and the Cameo hooks and eyes will serve you well, keeping the bodice fronts firmly and evenly joined.

After the waist is stitched, making even rows of stitching if the waist is to set straight, trim the seams evenly and overcast them, separating each in two parts, as they are to be afterward pressed open in the centre. Seams are cut in scallops and loosely overcast with silk; others are turned in and oversewed; others, again, are bound with thin lutestring binding, though all are occasionally clipped, to prevent any drawing when the seams are pressed. The first method is the easiest, and is now followed by the best of French and English dressmakers. Next press, using a bit of crinoline between the warm iron and lining. The featherboning and finishing the lower edge of the bodice will come next, and this is fully explained in Chapter VI. After turning up the edge face with a bias piece of silk or the dress goods, blindstitching each edge down, as in facing the wrist of a sleeve. If there is no outside vest or plastron on the centre front it is well to put a "blind" or "fly" down the left side of the front edge, to prevent any hint of the underwear showing through. This should be an inch wide, of the lining and the outside fabric, shaped like the edge, rounded over the bust and in at the waistline, and then stitched to the left front of the waist.

The belt should be set so that its lower edge is quarter of an inch above the waistline, to keep the bodice down at the back. This is featherstitched with silk twist at the centre back, side form and side gore seams, and when hooked in front should be a trifle tighter than the bodice, from which it takes the strain at the waistline. Use the best of dress shields to protect a dress from perspiration, and when sewing them on put the needle through the *covering* of the shield, not the rubber. Catch it in the armsize at each end and twice to the lining below, putting the back of the shield nearly to the side form seam, but making the shield come forward, not directly under the arm. Sew buttons on firmly with silk twist. Stitch silk and woollen bodices with M. Heminway & Sons' sewing silk and skirts with Clark's O. N. T. thread. Buttonholes in cotton waists are three-fourths of an inch apart and cut an eighth of an inch back of the edge. Silk belts worn with Griffon shirt waists or round fancy waists may be fastened to the skirt at the back with a gold or silver Clinton safety pin.

CHAPTER X.

FITTING UNUSUAL FIGURES.

A S PERSONS are not made according to a certain grade of measures, they are not fitted with one style of pattern or over one form of corset. It is now recognized that the corset has much to do with the fit of a gown, and some dressmakers go further and say that the corset, corset cover and petticoat should all be carefully fitted to the wearer before the dress waist is. The short, stout figure, the short but not stout woman, the very tall, thin figure and the woman that is very short and slender all differ from the ordinary figure, which weighs about 130 pounds, is five feet five inches in height, bust measure 36 inches and waist measure 24.

If the chapter on "Healthful Dressing" is read there can be no excuse for improper underwear, and the corset is now the important point. To get the correct fit in corsets, measure the waist outside of the dress and allow three inches, unless possessed of a very large abdomen, in which case only allow two inches less for the corset. A short, stout figure, having a very short waist, requires a corset with full bust, full hip measure and low under the arms, which requirements are to be found in the R. & G. brand, Nos. 716 and 399. The short figure that is not unusually stout or short waisted allows the same three inches difference in the waist measure, a 30-inch waist needing a 27-inch corset, and then selects No. 653 of the same make of corsets, remembering that a light-weight, flexible material will wear better and fit itself to the form more readily than any other.

Slender forms that are short and with a medium length of waist can wear No. 611 of the R. & G. corsets. Then the special long waist, No. 204, will recommend itself to those of a very long waistline with full hips and bust. The tall, thin figure, so often alluded to as a beanpole, needs a great deal of building up, but the result is worth the trouble. "As grace is the highest form of expression," aim to build up the form without giving the appearance of using artificial means, as to-day a woman who does not possess the necessary adjuncts for such improvement does not conform to the demand of the times. It is part of woman's mission to make herself as graceful as possible. All of this may be accomplished by the corset marked R. & G., No. 101, which has an extra long waist, with the bust cups narrow at the base, which permits the raising of whatever bosom the wearer may have. Do not lace the corset closely at the top, but leave it open, as usual, and fill in the front. Such a figure is flat under the arms, so commence padding at the centre front with curled hair covered in soft sateen, fitting the inside of the corset from a mere point near the steels to a crescent shape under the arms and narrow toward the back again. Arrange hip pads

of sateen and hair, shaping them to the corset, deepest over the middle of the hips and narrowing toward the centre, back and front. These must be tacked to the inside of the corset.

Use two flat laces, silk or linen, and lace both from the centre of the waistline, one up and the other down. For the first few days a corset should not be laced tightly; let it stretch a little and mold itself to the figure and then tighten the laces; but a corset should not be worn so tight that the wearer cannot feel her body move in it. When necessary alter the part over the hips, by the lower lace only. Do not use a rubber lacing, as it stretches the dress seams. A corset steel will not press into the wearer if the proper make of corsets for that particular figure is worn and laced properly. Do not buy an extra long-waisted corset imagining that you can grow to it.

A corset must fit the wearer and not the wearer squeeze herself to the shape of some certain corset. This brand of corsets alluded to never shows across the top outside of the dress if the proper measures are taken for the size of the corset. The boning does not run clear to the top, but stops an inch below, thus avoiding this common fault, and fits better for it as well. There are excellent corsets made nowadays for a dollar, but I would rather induce persons to pay a higher price, for the more light and pliable the corset the better the service.

The figures on the preceding page show the effect of proper fitting and dressing. On the right figure there is a full circular skirt, large sleeves, a round waist having a full plastron, a belt which only draws attention to the waistline and large revers, all being in bright colors. The hair is very fluffy around the face and makes it more moon-like than even nature intended. Her corset is too short waisted, and altogether the picture is not a happy one. The left figure has on a properly fitting R. & G. corset and her skirt is cut with eight gores, the many seams adding to the apparent height. The basque has a godet or fluted effect at the back and slopes away from a narrow pointed vest braided in lengthwise scrolls bordered by long, slender revers. The collar is not especially high, though of the crush or stock order, and the sleeves are moderately full. The hair is arranged in a high knot at the top, with only a small quantity curled on either side, showing a centre parting. All of the costume aims at giving length, and it is certainly a vast improvement on the second figure and shows what suitable and correct gowning will do.

Women of a short, full figure complain that the fashions are not made for them, which is true in a degree; but they must change the styles to suit their especial needs, which is easily accomplished after acquiring the necessary "know how." The Heath belt described in "Healthful Dressing" is excellent for stout women, as it reduces their apparent size and affords them a support as well. No size is added to the waistline, and the hips and abdomen are reduced. Belts add to the circumference of the waistline and should be abolished. Never despair of your figure; each and all may be improved, but only with the correct corset. In the chapter on "Cutting and Fitting Waists" directions are given for fitting the lining for very full or exceedingly slender persons.

CHAPTER XI.

MOURNING STYLES AND MATERIALS.

WITHIN the life of each of us comes the sorrowful time when mourning attire is necessary, and comparatively few know what fabrics should be used during this period or how they should be made up in order to be thoroughly correct. Good mourning, which of course includes crape, is very handsome and refined in its appearance, and, while the first outlay is seemingly expensive, the materials last a long time.

I always prefer Priestley's black goods, for their durability, variety and uniform black. It is an easy matter to know when you receive these fabrics as they are all stamped upon the selvedge with the firm's name. All of the materials mentioned are from this manufacturer. As black gowns are fashionable for those in and out of mourning, it is not an extravagance to buy them of good quality, as they can be cleaned and made over as no other fabric may be.

The deepest mourning is that worn by a widow, who dons Courtauld's English crape for at least a year. Her first dress should be of Eudora, which is a smooth, silk-warp material that may be spoken of as a perfected Henrietta. This latter name, however, has been so abused by using it for all-wool goods that it no longer means only a silk-warp fabric. Eudora more than fills its place, possessing a handsome lustre and feel and of a pure silk warp. This trims well with crape and should be made up in the prevailing fashion, without going to the extreme. A skirt, cape and basque usually form the first costume intended for street wear.

In using English crapes see that the crimps run from the left to right, diagonally. Even fine dressmakers sometimes err in making up crape on the wrong side. If cut on the bias crape will present straight lines; it is so pliable that it can be

44

shaped to any foundation and should be perfectly smooth, never puckered.

Such a trimming as crape should not be placed on the bottom of a skirt, where the hardest wear naturally comes. Folds set at least three inches above the edge are the only ones to be tolerated, and it is far better to put all such trimming on the

CRAPE.

Right Side.   Wrong Side.

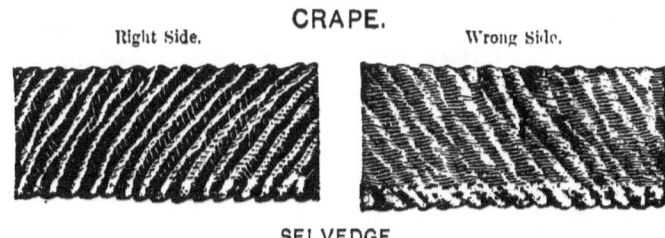

SELVEDGE.

basque in the shape of revers, a flat vest or full plastron, cuffs, high or crush collar, collarette, belt, etc., as Dame Fashion may dictate. The outside garment should be finished with crape folds on the edge, as a turnover collar and collarette.

For a time the use of crape dropped off, but during the past season it has again risen in favor, commencing in Paris and extending to Vienna, Berlin, London and the United States. Use it correctly and it will give you satisfaction, but never treat it as you would a hard twill serge, etc.

A widow's crape veil can be bought ready made, with woven hems or by the yard, and the hems blind-stitched down. When complete it should *at least* reach the waistline at the back, where the hem is three inches deep, and to the knees in front where an eight-inch hem is taken.

The small bonnet is covered plainly with crape, with milliners' folds on the edge, a white ruche inside and narrow black grosgrain ties. Over this the veil is draped and caught with dull jet pins on each side in small plaits.

At the end of six months or a year the veil may be unpinned and draped so as to hang in two layers at the back, with a small face veil of Brussels net edged with crape. Courtauld makes a waterproof crape that is excellent for general wear for both veils and dress trimmings. The silk-warp nun's veiling is also used for rainy days and travelling for both bonnets and veils, the latter being made and pinned on the bonnet in a similar manner to the crape.

A second dress for a widow, or any one wearing mourning,

should be of the silk-and-wool or all-wool Crape Cloth, which has the crimpy appearance of crape and makes up well alone or with crape. This is suitable for house or street wear and is often adopted by persons for the deepest mourning when they do not wear crape. Soleil is what I term a wool satin, as it has the gloss of this fabric combined with the softness of wool. For a handsome house gown in place of a mourning silk this makes up stylishly with crape, dull jet passementerie or lustreless silk.

Imperial serge furnishes the widow with a gown for general wear, made up with self-trimmings in the way of accessories and stitched edges. This is also worn by many ladies out of mourning. For warm weather the all-wool and silk-warp Clairette is as light as the traditional feather and also shakes the midsummer dust easily. The plainer gown for this time is of Tamise, a hard-twisted, durable material of light weight. A widow wears suède gloves as long as she is in deep mourning. During the second year she may wear black without crape and then put on quiet colors, though many wear crape for two years and plain black for one. Her bonnet for the latter time can be of straw or felt trimmed with black flowers, gros-grain ribbon, wings, etc.

A child wears deep mourning for a parent a year, or six months and lighter for a year, the same rule holding good for a parent wearing mourning for a child, a sister for a brother, a grandparent, etc. Nowadays people go from plain black into colors, but it is in better taste not to adopt the brightest shades at first. When wearing crape colors cannot be donned without a period devoted to plain black in the mean time. With the latter costume wear a face veil of net edged with English crape and suède or glacé kid gloves.

At this time white lisse can be worn in the neck and sleeves, and even with her first mourning a widow wears a turnover collar and cuffs of batiste or lawn, hemstitched. Pure white for house wear is considered correct in all mourning. Black and white piqué suits are worn in Summer with a white or black lawn shirt waist. Mourning has been defined as an outward mark of inward affection and respect and often prevents unkind remarks, as the wearing of crape at once tells the thoughtless inquirer that the wearer has suffered a loss which is at once respected.

CHAPTER XII.

COLUMBIA BICYCLE COSTUMES.

A HANDBOOK for the home dressmaker would prove incomplete without a chapter upon costumes to be worn by wheelwomen, who may be found in every city, town and village, gaining health and renewed youth in this delightful exercise. A neat costume and a perfect wheel are necessary, and for the latter there is but one recommended—the Columbia, which is dainty to look upon, light to move and absolutely flawless in its appointments and fittings. It is the universal favorite, and this season Model 41 is the one that every woman cyclist covets. There have been many pros and cons on the subject of bicycling, but the universal opinion is in favor of this now settled exercise. It exercises every muscle of the body, develops observation and a love of nature and sends the wheelwoman home after an hour or two of riding with a healthy appetite, cheerful spirits and an invigorated body. One cannot be melancholy and ride a Columbia bicycle; it is a universal panacea for the "blues"

Two handsome costumes are illustrated that are appropriately named Columbia, after the well-known wheel—one in the French bloomer style and the other with a short skirt, which is, of course,

more conservative. One of these suits is made of a cheviot in a rich brown shade—the jacket design—and the other of heavy serge in dark blue, both colors enduring dust and mud well, which must be met with occasionally. Both of these materials are cravenetted or rendered waterproof, thus being alike suitable for fair or stormy days. Fine and heavy serges and Imperial twills, as well as cheviots, are thus treated and stamped on the selvedge

every five yards with the word "Cravenette," as well as on the back of the material. Priestley's cravenettes are thus stamped, and have the firm's name as well. They are genuine, and in black and standard colors appropriate for a cycle costume as navy blue, gray, brown and green. These are the only colored goods made by Priestley.

Mounted on an attractive Columbia wheel is a fair rider

attired in the newest of Columbia bloomer suits. The bloomers, or Turkish trousers, can be fitted to a yoke or with four darts in front to a belt, with side plaits over the hips and at the back, making the garment gracefully full. At the lower end they are gathered to a band and buttoned just below the knee, the fullness falling several inches lower. These require 2¼ yards of goods 42 inches wide, using a width in each trouser leg. The leggins are of the same material, both articles being lined with silesia, fastened with tiny black buttons and the usual leather strap. They reach to the band of the bloomers and require three-quarters of a yard of 42-inch goods. The Norfolk jacket has three applied plaits in front, each stitched on the edges, with the centre one ending at the large revers. There are also three plaits at the back, with a turnover collar to the revers, besides a high collar and V of the goods, which can be made removable, so as to wear a linen chemisette occasionally. In the illustration a high turnover linen collar is worn and black tie. The large sleeves are plaited into the armholes and trimmed with a fold of the goods and small bone buttons, to imitate cuffs; similar buttons trim the inner edges of the two outer plaits. Belt of the cravenette serge, fastening with a buckle in front. The jacket is lined with silesia and boned in front, at the centre back, side seams and darts, though perfectly easy in fit and with very large armholes to admit of free use of the arms. This needs four yards of 44-inch goods. Black Oxford ties are worn having low heels, black hose and a blue straw sailor hat decorated with a folded crownband and upright loops of ribbon on either side.

A bicycle costume is not complete without a pair of Foster bicycle gloves, in brown, tan or any shade harmonizing with the costume. These gloves are of chevrette leather, stitched with saddlers' silk, well fitted and durable, with large hook fastenings that are convenient for the wheelwomen to quickly fasten or as quickly remove when the occasion arrives for it. They are stamped with the name inside of the wrist.

The figure dismounted by her Columbia bicycle has on a jacket suit of brown cravenetted twill, with a lighter shade of felt Alpine hat having a band and bow of ribbon, black ties and hose and a cotton shirt waist, with a leather belt. The leggins are of the same style as those on the other figure; the trousers are similar, only shorter, as they do not show. In fact, many ladies omit these with a skirt, but I find that experienced riders prefer them. These two garments need the quantities of material as given before. The cutaway jacket is lined with Nubian sateen, silesia or silk; has large armholes and is a close fit. It is cut in deep, square tabs all around, without extra fullness at the back, and has a rolled collar ending in tapering revers. The large sleeves are plaited in the armholes and have deep cuffs pointed to ard the outside, with a row of buttons down the outer edge. The short skirt is lined with silk or percaline, has a six-inch hem stitched in several rows, narrow front, back in two box plaits and three kilt plaits on each side, being not over three yards in width. Light-brown Foster bicycle gloves are worn with this Columbia suit, the jacket and skirt of which require 6½ yards of serge. Most of the skirts have on each side, three or four inches above the edge and 16 inches apart in front, a loop of silk elastic or a small brass ring, which is fastened to a button on the leggin, to keep the skirt from blowing. When mounting a wheel see that the skirt is not all pushed under, but leave sufficient in front to allow for the free motion of the legs. Short corsets must be worn, and tights are preferred to drawers. Seven inches from the ground is a good length for a skirt. Above all, sit straight on your wheel, and with the well-balanced seat of the Columbia bicycles this is an easy position to take.

CHAPTER XIII.

MATERNITY GOWNS.

THERE is a constant complaint among ladies that magazines do not pay sufficient attention to this style of costume, which must be worn, nevertheless. A gown for this purpose must be perfectly comfortable, look well—as I have said before, I believe in women dressing as well as their circumstances will allow—and also conceal the figure in a measure. The underwear should be the Mattelutz with black hosiery held by the Velvet Grip Hose Supporter, which will neither cut nor slip, fastening to the corset waist or to a shaped belt. This part of the toilette remains much as before, taking care not to wear it too heavy at any time. When pure wool is worn next to the body a very light weight will keep one comfortably warm and give less to carry around. The most important article comes next, viz., a comfortable, well-fitting corset waist that will keep the figure and add both to the appearance and health of the wearer. Use an Equipoise Waist, which is supported from the shoulders and combines two articles in one — the corset waist and a corset cover. Take a *tight* measure around the waist over the dress and get the same size. This waist is made for ladies, misses and children, and is perfectly adjusted to the figure. Being made of the best material the Equipoise Waist will outwear other corset waists.

Now put on white muslin drawers, made amply wide and finished with a yoke; these come just below the bend of the knee. Over these wear a short white muslin petticoat, on a yoke, and a corset cover or an equally short chemise; the latter garment is well fitted nowadays without fullness at the waistline, but the petticoat and corset cover take up less room. Now comes a second petticoat, of silk, alpaca, moreen, sateen, seersucker, etc., also made on a yoke, and it is a good idea to have these yokes made with a drawing string at the top, so that they may be enlarged as the occasion requires. During the Winter woollen drawers to match the vest and a flannel skirt on a yoke should be added, and dressed in this style the wearer is warm, free from bands, etc., and has no undue weight to carry. The Heath health belt is also recommended for wear at this time, worn attached to the outer petticoat. It keeps the figure in shape and gives the support now doubly necessary. It can be purchased attached to a silk petticoat that has a stylish flare or the belt is sold separate and sewed to any petticoat; but, of course, the skirt must be shaped to fit on the lower edge of the belt.

As for the dress itself there is usually provision made for a home gown, one for the street and one for nicer wear. The street suit should be of an inconspicuous color and either of a plain or small figured material. The indistinctly striped cheviots and Priestley cravenettes are excellent for this with velvet trimming. The skirt should be of a fashionable style, without trimming, interlined with haircloth to a depth of 10 to 20 inches and fitted to a yoke four inches deep at the top. Be careful to allow for any "hiking" or uplifting at the centre front. If the skirt is sewed to a band in preference the top of the front width should be curved up instead of down and sewed to the belt, with a few gathers in order to have an easy fit over the abdomen. Run a drawing string in the top of the yoke at the back or allow a large lap over on both yoke and band, to provide for their enlargement.

The sleeves can be of the reigning fashion and the waist take the form of a reefer jacket, which is a standard garment and one in good taste for all seasons. This will have loose, double-breasted fronts with an ample lap-over fastened with six large, handsome buttons. This has a centre-back, side-form and side-gore pieces, with the back flat, laid in a centre box plait or in three flutes called godets. This is one of the garments that you will certainly need a paper pattern for. The jacket should well cover the hips and abdomen, say seven inches below the waistline.

It can have a turnover collar and revers of velvet, leaving a V-shaped space to fill in with a linen or silk chemisette, or be cut high in the neck, with a straight or turnover collar of the A. W. B. Boulevard velvet. Line with silesia or sateen and interline the plaits or godets at the back as well as the collar and revers with haircloth. Make the lining and outside separate and turn the seams toward each other. Stitch the edges with M. Heminway & Sons' silk as a finish.

For morning wear a dressing sacque of striped flannel, flannelette, cotton goods, cashmere, etc., with an odd skirt or a loose wrapper, may be donned. For the afternoon nothing is neater or more comfortable than a teagown, which is one of the most convenient fashions that our English cousins ever sent over to us. This can be made with a close princess back or a flowing Watteau plait and close-fitting princess fronts, with a perfectly loose outer front of a soft contrasting material, as Japanese silk, crépon, etc. Under this front the lining hooks, leaving the centre to be lapped and hooked on the left side under the princess front of dress goods. The centre front is shirred or plaited to form a yoke, and a turnover or crush collar is attached. Large sleeves of the prevailing style. Ribbon bows, lace ruffles on the wrists, shoulders, down the front edges, etc., are permissible, as a teagown may be more or less trimmed, according to the taste and purse.

For dressy wear a silk or woollen gown should have a skirt similar to the one described for a cheviot gown and sleeves according to the prevailing style. For a waist there must be a full effect, to counteract the form. A slightly pointed short waist, to which a five-inch ripple piece is added (see chapter on waist accessories), has a good appearance if the fronts are flat and the full or ripple effect commences at the hips, continuing across the back. Have revers and crush collar of velvet or silk and add a loose plastron to drop over the waistline, which should be of soft silk, net, chiffon, etc., as it must be fluffy, but not bulky. Keep the skirt and waist closely connected at the back with the Clinton skirt supporter or safety pin, as a drooping skirt and lifted waist possess neither style nor comfort.

All of this style of dress is not of the so-called "dress reform" school, but it combines light weight, comfort, warmth, utility and a decent appearance, which traits many reform ideas do not include. I believe in reforming dress, inasmuch as health and comfort demand the above essentials, but I cannot see the need of making one's self look like a "guy," under any circumstances. At this trying time every woman wants comfort, and at the same time her natural good sense and modesty demand a gown that will render her less conspicuous, and these points are kept in view when describing costumes.

CHAPTER XIV.

DEFINITIONS NOT GENERALLY KNOWN.

THERE is a lack of understanding in regard to the glossary of terms used among dressmakers and well-informed dry goods men. As such words are constantly appearing in fashion writers' notes, many of whom are also ignorant of their meaning, I add a list of the terms, thinking them of interest to my readers:

Apron.—Any kind of a draped or flat skirt front.

Accordion Plaiting.—The finest of single plaits done by machinery; steamed and dried so as to retain their shape.

Ajour.—An openwork effect in embroidery.

Antique.—A word used to designate styles of former centuries, such as satin antique, moiré antique, etc.

Appliqué.—To apply one material to another, as lace applied to silk in a piece or single designs of leaves, a vine, etc.; also used as the name of a lace.

Arabesque.—A scroll figure.

Armure.—A fancy weave having a bird's-eye or diaper effect.

Astrakhan.—Fur of the Astrakhan goat; very wavy and short.

Baby Lamb.—Skin of still-born Persian lamb.

Bag or French Seam.—Seams stitched first on the right side and then on the wrong, leaving no raw edges.

Basque.—A tight-fitting waist extending below the waist-line in different shapes; after the dress of the Basque peasants of France.

Bayadère.—Stripes running crosswise of the goods.

Bengaline.—Applied to silk and woollen goods, as well as to

54

a small round cord filled with wool or silk. When the cord takes a fancy appearance the fabric is called crystal.

Bertha.—A trimming following the outline of a low-cut-neck dress, narrowing over the shoulders and made full, as a lace ruffle, or plain, as a shaped piece of velvet.

Beurre.—Butter color.

'Bishop Sleeve.—A shape like those worn on the robes of the bishops of the Episcopal Church; gathered at the top and again at the wrist into a straight cuff.

'Blazer.—A cutaway jacket extending below the waistline.

'Blouse.—Loose round waist.

'Boa.—Round fluffy article, long or short, for the neck; made of ribbon, lace or fur.

Bodice.—A tight-fitting waist.

Boléro.—A small round sleeveless jacket, after the style of the Spanish national costume.

Border.—Any trimming put on an edge or just above it.

Bouclé.—Tiny locks of hair scattered over the surface of a woollen fabric.

'Bouffant.—A very full effect.

'Bouillonnée.—A puffing.

Bourrette.—Rough threads or knots appearing as straight or broken stripes.

Bracelet Cuff.—A straight band around the arm.

Bretelle.—Sometimes called suspender trimming, as it extends from the shoulder—back and front or in front only—to the belt or edge of the bodice.

Broché (also written Brocade).—Resembling embroidery, though the effect is obtained by weaving.

Brodé.—Embroidered effects.

Cabochons.—Large jet, steel, pearl. etc., nailheads or brooches used in passementerie and for millinery.

Caracule.—Fine Astrakhan fur, looking as though it had been moiréd or watered.

Carreau.—A square or check figure.

Changeant and Chameleon.—Changeable effects from weaving two or three colors together.

Chiffon.—The softest thin silk material manufactured.

55

Chiné.—Effects obtained by printing the warp before weaving, making the filling then of a plain color.

Choux.—A large rosette like a cabbage.

Collarette.—Large collar of various shapes covering the shoulders.

Collet.—A small cape or large collar.

Crêpe Lisse.—A light silk fabric, very thin and transparent. but feeling like crape.

Crush Belt.—One of soft folds.

Cuirasse.—A perfectly plain, tight-fitting waist.

Cuir.—Leather colored.

Dresden.—Warp-print figures, like those used on Dresden chiné.

Drop Skirt.—A skirt of the dress material, made up separate from the lining and then hung or dropped from the same belt.

Duchesse.—The best satin fabric known.

Dutch Neck.—A square or round neck cut down only two inches below the throat.

Epaulette.—A trimming to fall over the shoulders.

Eton.—Short jacket after the style of the boys' uniform at the Eton school.

Façonné.—Fancy.

Faille Française.—A silken material having a soft cord.

Fichu.—A small cape, usually having long ends in front.

French Back.—A name applied to a single or double pointed yoke on a shirt waist.

French Gathers.—Gathers made of one long stitch on the outside and one underneath, and alternating.

Frogs.—Braid ornaments.

Full Back.—The straight back widths of a skirt gathered in two rows at the top.

Galloon and Passementerie.—Bead, silk, spangles, etc., dress trimmings.

Gauffré.—An effect seen in silk where the material is pressed into forms or patterns.

Gauntlet Cuff.—One shaped like the gauntlet on a riding glove modelled after the spreading cuffs on the ancient mailed gloves of knights.

Gigot.—Sleeves in a large puff at the top of the arm and close below.

Girdle—A cord, shaped belt or cincture for the waistline.

Glacé. – (See changeant.) When applied to kid gloves it means a smooth or dressed surface.

Godet.—Round or organ-pipe plaits or flutes, worn on skirts, basques and capes.

Gorget.—A high collar shaped low in front on the lower edge, like the collars of the coats of mail formerly worn by knights.

Granite.—An armure effect in both silk and woollen goods.

Gros Grain. Gros de Londres, Etc.—Small ribbed silk goods.

Guimpe.—Yoke of white or colored material usually worn by children.

Harlequin.—Of three or more separate colors.

Imprimé.—Printed.

Iridescent.—Rainbow, shot and changeable effects.

Jabot.—A trimming, usually of lace, which is gathered very full and allowed to fall as it will in shells.

Jardinière.—Color effects resembling a garden of flowers.

Lancé.—Small dots; also written *petits pois.*

Lapels.—See revers.

Leg-of-Mutton Sleeve.—One full at the top and close fitting at the wrist, shaped similar to a leg of mutton.

Liberty Satin.—A soft, lustrous satin.

Louisine.—A thin, soft silk.

Louis XVI., Regence, Directoire, Empire, Victorian, Colonial, Etc.—Styles that prevailed at certain periods in different countries.

Mélange.—A mixed effect of two or more colors.

Merveilleux and Rhadames.—Of the satin class of goods.

Miroir Velvet.—Looking-glass effects obtained by ironing.

Moiré.—A water effect like spreading waves over a silk, cotton or woollen surface.

Motif.—Part of a design, as a leaf from a spray of flowers.

Mousseline de Soie.—Transparent silk material.

Nacré.—Mother-of-pearl effects.

Natté.—The basket weave.

Natural Color.—The grayish flax shade known as "Natural," viz., undyed.

Ottoman.—A large rep or rib.

Oriental, Persian, Cashmere, Indienne.—Names applied to a series of colors and patterns formerly found on cashmere shawls.

Paillette.—Spangles of gelatine.

Plastron.—A full front to a waist.

Panache.—A cluster of short feathers.

Panel.—A straight or tapering piece set in the front or sides of a skirt, usually between rows of trimming, so as to give the idea of an inlay.

Peau and Poult de Soie.—Of the family of satins.

Placket.—The opening left at the side or back of a skirt.

Plait.—Knife plaits are narrow folds turned to one side; box plaits have a fold turned toward either side, and double and triple box plaits have two or three folds; kilt plaits are single folds turned one way.

Plumetis.—Printed and dotted fabrics.

Pointillé.—Dotted.

Polonaise.—A waist and overskirt combined in one garment; taken from the national costume of Poland.

Pompadour Effects.—Mixed colorings in light shades, as was worn in the time of Louis XV. and Mme. de Pompadour.

Postillion.—Flat back to a basque formed by extensions on the centre back pieces.

Princess.—A style of dress in which the waist and skirt are made in one-piece breadths from neck to feet.

Quadrillé.—Small checks or squares.

Quilling.—A narrow plait effect; a rose quilling is a very full triple box plaiting stitched through the middle, so as to have an effect like a row of full-blown roses.

Rain Fringe.—Single strands of beads fastened to a wide or narrow beading.

Rayé.—Striped.

Redingote.—An outside garment cut in princess style, with a skirt front beneath.

Revers.—Pointed or square pieces turned back or reversed, usually on the front of a waist.

Ruche.—A trimming of lace, silk, ribbon, etc., laid in plaits and stitched in the middle or toward one side.

Scintillante.—Changeable.

Shaped Bell.—One made of folds or a plain piece of material laid over a boned lining shaped to fit over the waistline and below it, being a little deeper in front than at the back where it rounds up according to the form.

Shirr.—Two or more rows of gathers having a space between.

Spanish Flounce.—A flounce extending fully half the depth of the skirt, gathered usually to form an erect ruffle.

Stock Collar.—A full collar or belt made of soft folds, in imitation of the stocks of 50 years ago, called crush collars and belts as well.

Strass.—Paste or artificial diamonds, also called Rhinestones.

Suède Kid.—Undressed kid; a skin from which the outer part has been rubbed off or skinned.

Surah.—A soft silk woven in nearly invisible cords.

Taffeta.—A smooth weave of silk.

Vandyke.—Pointed effects seen in laces, trimmings, etc.

Velour.—Velvet.

Vest.—A flat centre-front trimming for a waist and also a separate garment.

V-Shaped—An expression applied to a low-necked waist cut out in the shape of a V at the neck; also used to designate the shape of vests.

Watteau Fold.—A box plait down the centre of the back of a princess gown. which is laid only from the neck to the waistline and then hangs free.

Yoke.—A trimming of a square, round or pointed shape for the chest and shoulders.

Zibeline.—Woollen material having long hairs.

CHAPTER XV.

APPROPRIATE COLORS AND MATERIALS.

WHAT to wear to improve one's appearance and to disguise one's poor points is a bit of knowledge sought for by many. I cannot claim to make all beautiful, but I do know from the best of teachers—experience—that any woman can be improved by a tasteful selection of shades and dress fabrics.

A short, stout figure must not wear bright colors, a plaid, wide stripes or large designs. Narrow stripes, tiny patterns or very small checks will, however, cause such a person to look more slender than a plain material, unless it is black. Rough materials must not be even looked at by such a figure for fear that the possessor might be tempted to buy them, and then regret it as long as the dress lasted.

A stout woman that is tall has an easier task in dressing her figure, as it only requires condensing in width. Narrow and medium stripes (ditto figures), checks and plain goods may be used in dark and light shades. Avoid a mass of white, and if a white gown is worn during the Summer, white being appropriate for all ages, select a ribbed piqué or a corded dimity.

Short, slender women can wear any color, but their lack of height prevents immense plaids, wide stripes and very large designs from being just what they want. The happy medium is better in every respect here in styles and designs. One thing to be remembered is that too broad effects cannot be successfully carried off by a woman under 5 feet 4 inches, no matter what the reigning fashions may be.

The tall, not-too-slender woman of about 5 feet 6 inches, and weighing 140 pounds, is the one that it is a delight to dress, especially if she has a good walk, round waistline and long waist. This lucky woman can wear anything, but she is not often found.

The very slender woman of more than medium height is now in the best of luck, for all the fashions just suit her. She can even wear tiny stripes, because the *bouffant* style of dress will counteract this material.

Let her indulge in flaring skirts, large sleeves, big collarettes, round waists, full-skirted coat basques, crush collars and fluffy trimmings. A full ruff of two-inch lace turned over the top of a crush collar w ll soften the longest face in existence.

It is no idle vanity to study your needs and enhance your good points, unless carried to excess and important duties neglected, too much extravagance engendered and selfishness cultivated therefrom.

In regard to shades for different complexions there is much to be learned, but a few general rules can be followed by every one. So many of my correspondents through the *Ladies' Home Journal* (I do not answer personal letters through any other medium) ask what colors will suit their hair. Now, the hair is a secondary consideration, except it be a carroty red.

The complexion is the first guide; then the hair and eyes. The skin with a color can wear what the same degree of fairness without a rosy flush could not touch. Then some complexions have color at night and not during the day, and all of this must be thought of when buying an evening gown. Others can wear a color, like navy blue, which is unbecoming alone, but if a touch of pink or red is put with it the whole effect is pleasing.

Navy blue has an old effect upon any skin, except a fresh, rosy blonde, and brings out lines hitherto invisible to any eyes; but combine pink, cardinal or gold with it and the entire effect is different. Some people claim that they cannot wear black, but as black is always in good style and forms the most convenient gown for all occasions, it is well to know that all ages, sizes and complexions can wear it by using a becoming color next to the face.

Velvet is the most becoming of materials, then soft, woollen goods, figured silks, plain silks, figured cottons, and finally plain cotton goods. Lace has a softening effect, especially in cream shades.

What is known as a brune blonde (neither light nor dark) can wear almost any color, but if sallow steel gray, clear white, navy blue, brick red, yellowish green and grayish tan must be avoided. A clear, light blonde can wear anything but light red, gold, deep pink, reddish purple and yellowish brown. Very dark red and mauve are becoming to every style of blonde complexion.

Red-haired women usually have clear complexions, but from the nature of the hair let them flee from emerald green, yellow, pink, light red, light purple, golden tan and pinkish gray. Black, cream, pale and dark green, light and navy blue, violet, turquoise, gray and nut brown are becoming for the Titian-red locks, as well as deep coppery-red tints.

The rosy brunette may wear with satisfaction cream, pale blue, pink of every shade, ditto red, clear and reddish purple, yellow of every shade, navy blue combined with pink or red, brown of every tint, pinkish gray, ditto mauve, and dark green. A sallow brunette needs warm tones to supply the rosy flush denied by nature. Let her avoid all blues, gray, violet, green and white. Yellow, orange, deep and rose pink, bright and dark red, golden and reddish browns and reddish purple are the shades for such a skin. Black is also becoming when combined with pink or gold.

Old rose is rather a *passé* color just now, but it is lovely for all that and combines beautifully with black, gray, white and brown. It can be worn by a drab blonde, brune blonde, rosy and sallow brunette. By the way, I wonder how many realize that sallowness comes chiefly from a torpid liver, and if proper food, frequent bathing and plenty of exercise are adopted much of the sallowness will disappear? Exposure to all sorts of weather without a veil also roughens and yellows the skin, but its worst enemy is a dormant liver.

An old test to discover what is becoming to the skin is to put the ungloved hand by the color, and if it looks well the face will. This loses force when we remember that many have whiter hands than complexions, and *vice versa*. Another plan is to dress in a shade that exactly matches the eyes, but this restricts the wardrobe to one color, and such gowns lack the spice of variety said to be necessary for our well being. Find out what is becoming, and then cling to those shades, be they three or six. In these days of combinations of colors and materials many changes may be rung upon even three colors for the groundwork. It costs no more to dress becomingly than to make a "guy" of yourself, and in the former case you will be happier, and thus diffuse more happiness around you.

CHAPTER XVI.

HEALTHFUL AND STYLISH DRESSING.

IT SEEMS to be the fad of many writers and talkers to prate of all fashionable gowning as being unhealthy, as though health and homeliness grew like twin cherries upon the same stalk. Fortunately, many women do not dress in a manner calculated to injure their health, but some always did so and probably will continue in the same path, but in the mean time the race is improving, and, as a rule, women dress in a more healthful manner now than since the days of the classically garbed Grecian maiden.

Health is the greatest blessing Providence can bestow upon a woman, yet there is sufficient original sin in human nature to implant the desire within the heart of every woman to look stylish and to dress becomingly as well as healthfully. The essence of style is a birthright and cannot be imparted, but proper materials and designs and becoming colors will give a gown a certain amount of style, especially if combined with a modicum of originality. As a general rule, do not anticipate fashions; neither be too modest and fail to grasp an opportunity to have a pretty, stylish gown, which gives the wearer a feeling of universal good fellowship with her sisters and adds to her confidence and happinesss.

In selecting a stylish, healthful attire, commence at the very foundation and wear well-fitting underwear. I thoroughly believe in pure wool being worn next to the skin, and especially when one is subject to colds, etc. For this reason I suggest the "Mattelutz" steam-shrunk sanitary underwear, a vest and drawers or a combination suit of pure wool or a mixture of wool and cotton. These garments have a delightful feeling of softness and warmth without weight and are well fitted, thus not adding to the apparent size of the figure, and they carry out the principle of a combination of light weight and warmth. The "Mattelutz" steam-shrunk underwear is easily kept soft and in perfect shape if properly washed. Soak it for forty minutes in a suds made of Ivory soap and water as warm as the hands can endure; a little ammonia may also be added. There is economy and convenience as well in using this soap for such a purpose, as it floats, and is thus ever in sight when needed, in place of melting away under the water. Cleanse by drawing through the hands, but *do not rub* on a washboard. Rinse in lukewarm water, and either force out the water with a clothes wringer or squeeze between the hands. Do not twist the pieces dry. Lay each piece out flat to dry and iron on both sides while slightly damp. The all-wool and cotton-and-wool underwear should be thus washed.

Now comes the one article that is ever a bone of contention—the corset; yet this much-abused piece of womanly attire brings comfort, health and style in its wake if properly applied. If a corset is of a proper fit it will feel comfortable and cannot injure the wearer. If it does not fit that is your fault, and not the corset's. I have told my readers in the different chapters on "Fitting Unusual Figures" and "Maternity Gowns" how to select a corset or corset waist as one may prefer. These instructions have been revised by an expert corset fitter, so no one can do better than to follow them. Remember that when you cannot feel your body move in a corset when bending that it is too tightly laced, and this I most strongly oppose. There is no pressure unless the lacing is wrong or the corset incorrectly fitted to you. Remove these difficulties and you will have an improved form and health as well.

As for hosiery, every well-dressed woman knows that black stockings are universally worn. Those stamped "Louis Herms-dorf, Dyer," will be found most satisfactory, for all grades of hosiery thus dyed have the same care and show the same stainless result, making the manufacturer a benefactor of the human race. Personal experience is the best teacher, and I have worn stockings of this dye for years without one pair ever crocking the clothes, staining the flesh or fading when washed. I have yet to hear of a pair of the genuine Hermsdorf black dye hose proving the contrary. This explains why black stockings are now worn by both sexes so much and upon all occasions by children and adults. The stockings are kept up by a hose supporter that may be fastened to the side of the corset or be attached to the regularly fitted belt, as the supporters are of both styles. The garter is so injurious in stopping the circulation of the blood, if worn sufficiently tight to keep the stocking smooth, that I need not say anything of its disadvantage.

The shoes must be selected according to the shape of the feet, as one may wear with comfort pointed toes, while the next comer can only walk with the broad toes and low heels. I must draw attention to the fact that low ties on the street, however, require overgaiters on a cool day or stiff ankles and a severe cold may follow the exposure. Lace all shoes firmly over the instep, to keep the foot from pushing forward.

In the matter of muslin underwear there are many minds regarding chemises *versus* underpetticoats and corset covers. The two latter take the place of the former and show less fullness at the waistline. Stout figures may have drawers and petticoat fitted to a deep yoke with a drawing string from the side. Do not put buttons on a piece of underwear, except corset covers, unless you wish them to show through the dress at the waistline. Both stout and thin figures can wear the Heath Health Belt which w ll improve their appearance, afford a support and reduce obesity. I know that practical ideas have generally been omitted in the belts sold for this purpose, but this one is indorsed by physicians and is extremely practical in all its details. The belt may be had separate from the skirt or attached to a silk petticoat. In the former case it can be sewed to any skirt, or it is worn over all of the petticoats without attaching one to it. Unlike all other belts it is not worn up around the waistline, but fits over the hips. It is boned so as to support the abdomen, and being made up with elastic and peculiarly fitted it remains in position when the wearer is sitting or walking. When a woman is obliged to be on her feet much or is unduly stout such a belt becomes an absolute necessity to her.

With light-weight wool drawers, a cambric petticoat, flannel petticoat, and then a silk, alpaca, sateen, etc., petticoat sewed to one of these belts, or to a deep yoke, one can be warmly dressed and yet not have any heavy weight to be dragging over the hips. The upper part of the body will be sufficiently clothed with the woollen vest, corset and corset cover. If a chemise is preferred, omit the short petticoat and corset cover, wearing the corset next to the undervest. There is nothing particularly reforming about this style of dress, but it is light and warm and will be comfortable to wear. Let your dress skirts be cut short enough not to touch the ground when walking. Never have them of very heavy material; interline them with haircloth of a light weight, and line with Nubian fast black percaline. A skirt can be of a fashionable cut without being extremely wide, and every half yard adds to the weight. Use a Clinton skirt supporter to keep the skirt firmly attached to the waist at the back, as it removes the weight from the hips and keeps the skirt of an even length all around without any sagging at the centre back.

Many ladies of a stout figure prefer woollen tights to drawers, as they are a closer fit. Then they can also have their silk, alpaca or sateen petticoat lined with flannel attached to a Heath belt and omit the flannel petticoat, thus reducing the number of yokes to be worn and the quantity of skirts at the same time. If a petticoat is three yards wide, trimmed with a 10 or 15 inch ruffle, and has a velveteen binding with featherbone run in it, the skirt will be held out and the petticoat never flap around the ankles. A flannel-lined silk or sateen petticoat sewed to a Heath belt and tights need be the only articles around the hips of a stout figure besides her corset. She can also wear a low-neck, sleeveless Swiss ribbed undervest for a corset cover, as it fits itself over the corset without a particle of fullness.

Do not wear a long, heavy cloak when walking, as it flaps around the ankles so as to impede progress and proves a dead weight from the hips down. If the legs are cold warm them with woollen drawers, and not with heavy dress skirts and long wraps. Keep the extremities warm and the dress light and do not follow the extremes of fashion, for they cannot fail to interfere with health. In the mean time, keep up with the reigning fashions, but adapt them to your especial needs. Just how to do this is one of the aims of this little book, as I claim that every woman should be garbed becomingly and healthfully; it costs no more, will prove a rational manner of dressing and render the world more refined and artistic.

Well-fitting gloves round out a stylish toilette for any occasion. If for travelling, shopping or outing, a piqué glove is advisable, as it is of a heavier kid and has a tailor-like finish that is especially suitable for such costumes. For visiting and dressy wear a fine glacé kid is recommended in tan, brown, gray, mode, white, etc. Both styles have the new large Foster hooks and are to be recommended for their utility and convenience. They readily fasten and unfasten; do not wear out the fingers and patience, and can be made to fit any size of wrist. Do not cultivate the habit of buying cheap kid gloves, for one pair at $1.50 will usually outwear two pair of the $1 grade, and look better as well. It is worth while having a glove that is well-fitting, durable and convenient to fasten, as no other article adds more to the general finish of a stylish toilette, and I have found this make of gloves worthy of this reputation.

66

CHAPTER XVII.

TO RENOVATE MATERIALS.

PARTLY worn silks, dress goods, laces, ribbons, velvets, etc., may be renovated and made over in these days of combinations of fabrics and colors in a manner to delight an economical woman. Do not try to make over anything too old to repay you, and from the beginning remember that unless the work is done with care it will not be worth the time spent upon it. If you have really handsome goods to be dyed or cleaned I would advise sending them to a professional dyer, as they can, of course, get results far beyond the housewife. Such a house as Lewando's can make a renovated material look like a piece of new goods, following the French method, which is considered the best in the world. Two old gowns may often be dyed together and one new dress evolved from them. Badly faded goods will not dye well in bright colors; all colors dye black nicely. The colors that cover fading and staining the best in dyeing are black, brown, green, olive, plum and maroon. Crape can be refinished to look like new and made as near waterproof as can be expected. If, however, the cleaning must be done at home remember it is apt to roughen the hands, necessitating the use of a vegetable oil soap, like the Ivory, to counteract all such effects.

First rip up each article, using a penknife or small pointed scissors; pick out all the threads and shake each piece. Then brush woollen goods with a whisk and dust silk, ribbon, velvet or bead trimming by rubbing with an old silk handkerchief. Put the buttons, ribbons, laces, etc., in boxes properly marked and tie up the different materials in separate packages, ready for the cleaning, dyeing or sewing, as it may be. I cannot advise any one to use old linings, as, when washed, they will shrink out of shape and size, and it is impossible to fit or hang a dress properly unless the linings are cut exactly right, as I have explained in the chapters on cutting and fitting. Wash and iron the linings taken from partly worn gowns, if they are worth it, and keep to use for children's frocks, which they will cut down to.

In using any cleaning fluid remember that benzine and naphtha are *very explosive* when brought in contact with fire. Benzine sometimes leaves a stain like water. Always try a piece of the material to be cleaned first, to see the effect. When sponging a fabric do it with downward strokes and use a wad of the same material or similar to it.

A good quality of black silk cleans well and repays one for careful handling. If too shabby to make up as a dress use it for a petticoat. If worn for the latter garment be sure and put ruffles of taffeta on it, for no other silk has the same stand-out tendency as taffeta. Have a clean, smooth table to sponge your silk upon, and rub on the surface that will be worn out. Here are several fluids for sponging black silk, and all are excellent: Equal parts of warm water and alcohol; cold coffee, made strong and well strained; stale beer; water in which an old black glacé kid glove has been boiled, using a pint of water to a glove and boiling it down to half of that quantity. Cut the selvedge here and there of each straight width, to prevent any drawing. Hang each piece on a line to drip nearly dry, and then iron on what will be the wrong side with a moderately warm iron, putting a piece of thin black crinoline between the iron and silk. Lay the pieces away without folding them.

A very hot iron often discolors silk. If a white silk handkerchief was ironed with a cold iron, and with a linen handkerchief between the iron and silk, the latter would not yellow. Clean black ribbons as you do silk. Clean colored silk with water in which a kid glove the color of the silk has been boiled, using a new tin pan to boil it in; strain and add a little hot water and ammonia. Wash in this and put half a teaspoonful each of borax and spirits of camphor to a quart of the rinsing water and hang each piece up until it dries, but do not iron. Another authority says that ribbons should be washed in a lather of cold water and Ivory or any other perfectly pure soap, and should be ironed while damp, using a cloth under the iron. To remove the creases from silk dip each piece in a bath of naphtha and hang up to dry. Any unpleasant odor is removed by hanging articles thus cleaned in the open air.

A good black woollen gown should be in every wardrobe,

for its utility, general convenience and fashionable qualities, and such goods as serge, cheviot, cashmere, Henrietta, etc., are easily cleaned. First remove the grease spots with naphtha, remembering that this fluid is very explosive when exposed to either a lamp or fire. If your black goods are of a rusty color send them to Lewando's to be redyed. Clean mud and ordinary spots from a black dress with a rag of the same wet with warm water and ammonia. Never rub on the washboard a silk or woollen fabric that is being renovated, nor wring it tightly by twisting in the hands: either put it through a wringer or pat it nearly dry between the hands. To clean black goods make a lather of warm soapsuds, using a good soap without free alkali, like the Ivory, as a strong soap will ruin the goods, and a teaspoonful of borax to every two quarts of water. Into this dip the goods up and down and wash between the hands; then wring gently and pat partly dry; hang in the shade, and when nearly dry iron on the wrong side with a moderately warm iron. Always rinse once in lukewarm water, and iron until the material is perfectly dry. Wash alpaca in the same manner as above, adding a little gum-arabic to the rinsing water.

Remove grease from colored cashmere with French chalk. Rub it on the spot, then let it remain overnight, and in the morning brush off; if necessary repeat the treatment. Wash a colored woollen fabric, as cashmere or serge, in warm water, putting a teaspoonful each of beef's gall and ammonia to a pail of water. Have the rinsing water ready, with a small portion of beef's gall in that, and wash and rinse quickly; dry in the shade and iron on the wrong side with a warm — not hot — iron. French chalk can be used on any color and material. Benzine will remove paint—it is very explosive—and if it leaves a stain like water it may often be removed with French chalk. Grease is also removed by rubbing the spot with a lump of wet magnesia and after it is dry brushing off the powder. Remove all grease spots before further cleaning a piece of silk or woollen goods.

The best cleaners are the French people, and they do not advise ironing lace, but if it is done have the ironingboard well padded and put a cloth between the lace and iron. Do not dry black lace by the fire or it will turn rusty. Wash black lace in a pint of warm water with a teaspoonful of borax dissolved in it, and use an old black kid glove for a wad to sponge it with. Borax, diluted alcohol, beer, strained coffee, and water in which a black kid glove has been boiled, are all excellent renovators for black laces, as is also cold strained green tea. White cotton laces are washed in a warm Ivory soapsuds, rinsed, boiled, rinsed for the second time, patted nearly dry, and then pinned down on a clean towel over a smooth bed or pillow. Every point of the scallops must be carefully pinned down into shape. Lace that has yellowed from age may be whitened by covering it with the same soapsuds and allowing it to stand in the sun. Grated breadcrumbs will clean lace that is not much soiled. The French dyers referred to renovate lace as beautifully as they do silk and woollen dress materials. They also mend laces of all kinds and restore real laces as well.

A creamy écru shade may be given to white lace by putting strained coffee or powdered saffron in the rinsing water until the color is obtained. All laces should be soused up and down and gently squeezed or clapped dry between the hands. White silk laces are cleaned by soaking them in milk overnight, then they should be washed in warm Ivory soapsuds, rinsed, pulled out, and finally pinned down on a towel while damp. Delicate laces are also cleaned with calcined magnesia. Spread the lace on clean white paper, sprinkle both sides of it with magnesia, place a second piece of paper over it, put it away between the leaves of a large book for a few days, and finally shake off the powder. Gold and silver laces are cleaned with grated breadcrumbs mixed with powdered blue. Sprinkle this well-mixed preparation over the lace for a few hours, then brush off the crumbs with a piece of flannel and rub the metal gently with a piece of red velvet, the color of which is as important as the material, though why this is so no one can tell, unless it is some property of the red dye.

White crocheted shawls are cleaned by covering them for a night with flour or white cornmeal; then shake them well, and if not perfectly clean repeat the treatment. The stockinet and good rubber dress shields can be washed in warm suds made with Ivory soap, which is pure, pulled into shape, and dried by pinning them up in a window. Japanese, China and pongee silks and handkerchiefs should be washed in warm water, rinsed at once and dried in the shade. When nearly dry iron with a cloth between the silk and iron. Soak genuine whalebones, when bent, in warm water, and then at the end of thirty minutes iron them out with a hot iron. Navy-blue flannel dresses should be washed in bran and water without any soap, but with a cup of salt to set the color. Soft water is always the best for cleaning, or hard water may be softened with a little borax or ammonia. When jet passementerie looks dusty and rusty wipe it off with a wad of black silk or cashmere dipped in diluted alcohol, and finally wipe dry with a clean rag.

Remove grass stains with alcohol, which seldom spots even the most delicate color. They can be removed from muslin with molasses. In each case keep covering the stain until it fades out.

A cleansing fluid that has been very highly recommended to me by a practical woman pharmacist is made as follows: Gasoline, one gallon; ether, one teaspoonful; chloroform, one teaspoonful; ammonia, two teaspoonfuls; alcohol, one gill. Mix well, and do not use near a fire or in a closed room. Do not use the last half cupful if cleaning delicate colors, as the ammonia settles and will discolor light fabrics. Buy the last four drugs in quantities of an ounce, as it will be cheaper in the end, and keep for future use what is not needed at once.

This fluid cleanses silk and woollen materials and does not shrink the fabric, leaves a new finish, does not yellow white, can be used on the most delicate colors and fabrics, and is very cheap. Pour out sufficient of the fluid to cover the article to be cleaned, using a china washbowl or new tin pan. Put the article in and wash as you would in water, rubbing the soiled spots especially with an old soft toothbrush on a flat surface. Wring out from this and rinse in a second portion of the fluid; wring out again and hang in a draught until the fluid evaporates. Save the remaining fluid as it can be used a second time on dark materials, like men's clothes, black dresses, carpets, etc. If the article is too large to put into the fluid use a sponge or cloth similar in color to the soiled fabric. This cleanser will not remove stains made by syrup or sweets, which must first be washed in water.

There is a waterproof crape for wearing in damp weather, but if the ordinary crape is worn and gets rusty and slimsy, as it will in time, it can be renovated at home after a formula that I have personally tested many times. Rip out the hems of veils, brush away all dust with an old silk handkerchief, and wind the crape smoothly, catching it with pins, around a broomstick or clothesstick. Fill the washboiler half full of water, and when it boils lay the stick across it, the ends resting on the edge lengthwise. Keep the water boiling hard and steam the crape all day, turning the stick so that every part of the crape may be reached. Then put the stick away for twenty hours, as the crape must be perfectly dry before unpinning it. This will make it retain a good black color and it will be crisp to the touch.

When black or colored velvet has the pile crushed and is creased, it can be easily renovated at home. Have a pan of boiling water on the stove, and over this hold the wrong side of the velvet. Let it be thoroughly dampened with the steam, and then induce a second person to assist you in the good work by brushing the right side of the velvet with a whisk, stroking the pile up briskly until it seems capable of standing alone; then lay that piece aside to dry and take another one. White ostrich feathers are cleaned with flour or naphtha, and all are easily dyed black. They are curled by first heating them slightly, and then curl each flare over a dull knife; but if near a feather curler I would advise patronizing her, as the professionals do it far better than any amateur can. When feathers are worn in the rain or damp they should be dried at once over the stove, which generally restores the curl.

White and light-colored kid gloves are cleaned on the hands with naphtha—remember its explosive qualities until the gloves are perfectly dry. Put on one glove and rub it with a clean piece of white flannel dipped into naphtha; wet it all over, and then rub nearly dry with a second piece of flannel. Do the second glove in the same manner, and let them remain on the hands until dry, in order to retain the shape; then hang in a window until the odor has left. A sachet bag of white rose and orris-root powder in your glove box will keep gloves delightfully perfumed.

There is but One
Perfect Interlining.

THAT IS

HAIR CLOTH.

∴ This is the only
∴ Stiff, Elastic and
∴ Resilient Interlining
∴ made, and it has
∴ proven itself a

"Survival of the Fittest."

We Are the Best and Largest Manufacturers of Hair Cloth in the World.

The Fashionable Flare Effect in Skirts can only be obtained with Hair Cloth.

STANDARD HERRINGBONE for Skirts
Styles 10 4, 14/4, 10/5, 20 5, in Grey or Black.

PLAIN OR FRENCH for Skirts and Sleeves.
Styles 84 3, 98/3, 146/3, 170 3, 206/4, in Grey, Black or White.

Write us for samples and remember, "There Is No Substitute" and the "Best Is the Cheapest."

AMERICAN HAIR CLOTH COMPANY,
CHARLES E. PERVEAR, Agent,
PAWTUCKET, R. I.

74

Home Dressmaking

cannot be done without a good

We can furnish you with Original French Fashions in a medium size for from

✄　✄　✄　✄　**25**^{C.} Up　for each pattern.

SIZES.—30-inch bust ; 41-inch length for skirts and 24-inch waist.

Made=up Paper Patterns for Dressmakers.

The leading Fashion Journal is

L'Art de la Mode,

Per Year, - $3.50
Six Months, $2.00　} Postage Free.

Single Numbers, 35c.
Send 2-cent stamp for Sample Copy.

containing only the Latest and Original Designs.

PUBLISHED MONTHLY BY

The Morse=Broughton Company,

3 East 19th Street, New York.

THE HEATH HEALTH BELT.

It is sold separate from the petticoat.
Can be applied to any petticoat.

It Is a
Boon to
Every
Woman.

Once Worn
Will Not
Be Discarded.

It Reduces
Obesity.

It Affords
Abdominal
Support.

It Removes
That Tired
Feeling.

It Gives a
Better Fit to
the Skirt.

Is Practical
and
Healthful.

With a Silk Petticoat, in colors or black, this Health Belt is from $10 to $25.

The Belt Alone Is $5.00.

This belt is endorsed by **Physicians**
and by **Every Woman** wearing one.

Sole Maker and Patentee,

Mrs. MARY HEATH,

114 FIFTH AVENUE, NEW YORK.

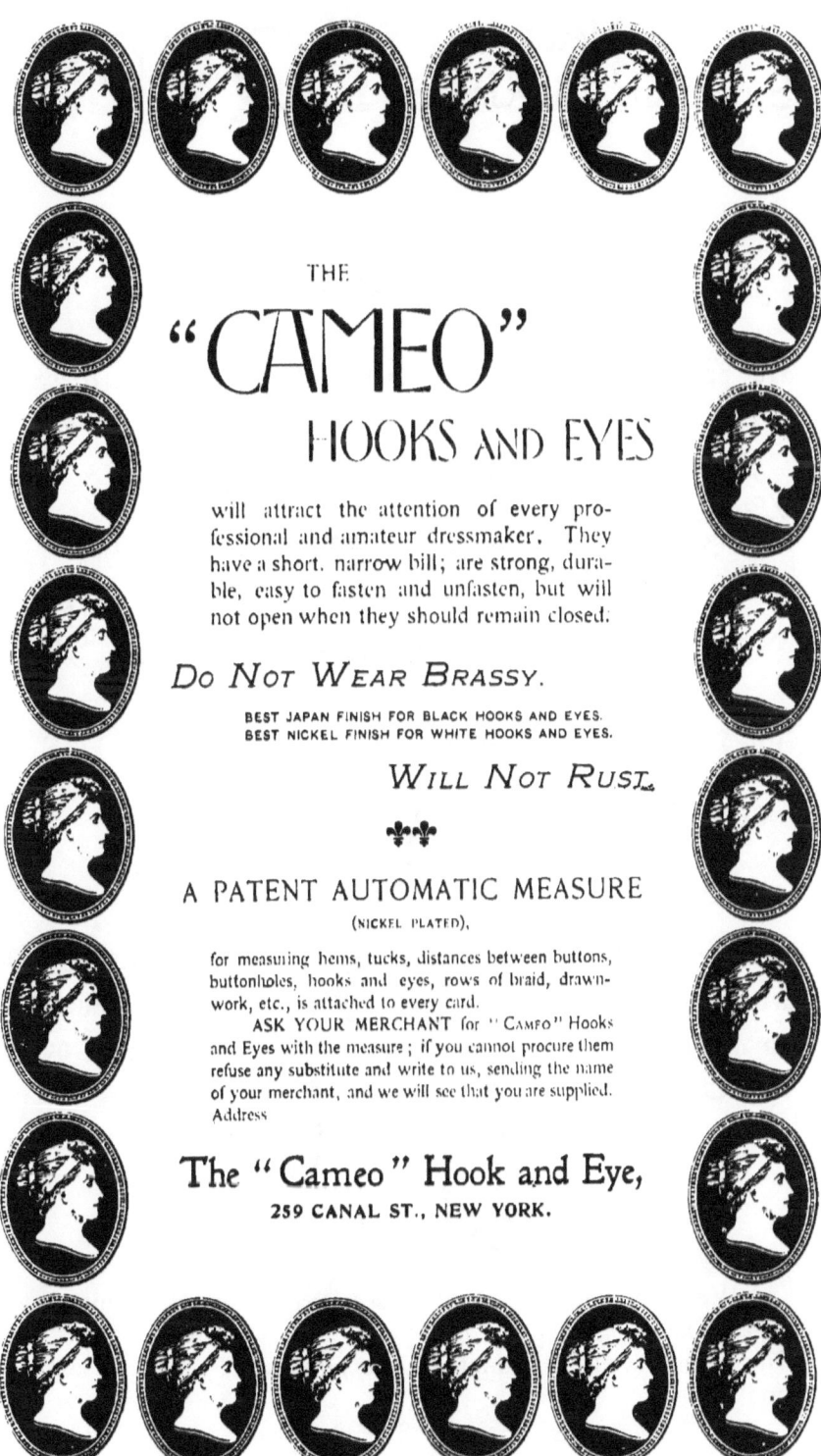

THE

"CAMEO"

HOOKS AND EYES

will attract the attention of every professional and amateur dressmaker. They have a short, narrow bill; are strong, durable, easy to fasten and unfasten, but will not open when they should remain closed.

DO NOT WEAR BRASSY.

BEST JAPAN FINISH FOR BLACK HOOKS AND EYES.
BEST NICKEL FINISH FOR WHITE HOOKS AND EYES.

WILL NOT RUST.

❖

A PATENT AUTOMATIC MEASURE

(NICKEL PLATED),

for measuring hems, tucks, distances between buttons, buttonholes, hooks and eyes, rows of braid, drawnwork, etc., is attached to every card.

ASK YOUR MERCHANT for "CAMEO" Hooks and Eyes with the measure; if you cannot procure them refuse any substitute and write to us, sending the name of your merchant, and we will see that you are supplied. Address

The "Cameo" Hook and Eye,

259 CANAL ST., NEW YORK.

The New
Street and Bicycle GLOVES

MADE BY

Foster, Paul & Co

are practical, durable and well fitting, and bear these brands :

PRICE,

$1.50

Per Pair.

They are sold by leading dry goods firms of the U. S.

Perfect=fit=
with improved
do not catch
cidentally un=

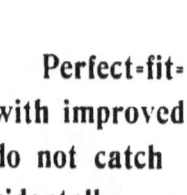

ting wrists,
hooks, which
in lace or ac=
fasten.

When buying Kid Gloves see that they are stamped : "Manufactured by Foster, Paul & Co." or "Foster's Patents." This assures well-fitting and durable gloves and improved large hooks.

Three Indispensable Articles.

The Clinton Skirt Supporter

Which is readily adjusted and keeps the waist and skirt from becoming separated.

This recommends itself to every woman wishing to have a neat, stylish appearance when wearing a round waist.

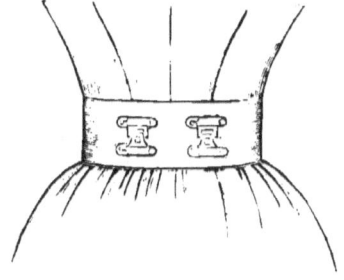

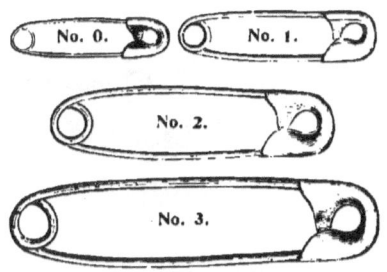

The Clinton Safety Pin.

Made in rolled gold, sterling silver, nickel plate and black. This is the best constructed and most desirable Safety Pin ever made.

The Best Pins for Dressmaking and Personal Use.

Sharp points and won't bend.

An absolute necessity for every woman sewing.

All of the leading merchants have these goods, or apply to

The Oakville Company,

NEW YORK OFFICE,
49 HOWARD ST.

WATERBURY, CONN.

Half of the Success in Home Sewing

IS IN USING A

Perfectly Reliable Thread.

This can be secured by asking for

FOR ..

Hand and Machine Sewing

It remains unsurpassed.

It is wound on White Spools.

Needles are equally important.

If you have not used

Milward's Helix Needles

You have missed much comfort in sewing.

FOR SALE EVERYWHERE.

The One Brand of Fast Black Cotton Dress Linings for Both the Waist and Skirt

IS THE

Nubian

It WILL NOT STAIN OR CROCK the flesh or underwear, and always remains the same unchangeable, reliable black. 🙥 🙥 🙥 🙥

The MOIRÉD PERCALINE has the rustle and appearance of silk for a small cost; the stiff-finished CAMBRIC ranks next for SKIRT linings. 🙥 🙥

For a WAIST try the soft-finished percaline or silesia, or sateen, and they will be fit for the handsomest gown.

Such a lining adds to the style of a costume.

Look for this on every yard of the Selvage.

Nubian Fast Black

All Leading Dry Goods Stores.

82

STRONG—ELASTIC—DURABLE.

Our Bones and Methods are Invaluable in the Dressmaking Art.

SEE US DEMONSTRATE AND BE CONVINCED.

 BONES AND METHODS CHEERFULLY SHOWN
AT ANY OF OUR DRESS BONING PARLORS.

Dressmakers and others who are interested are cordially
invited to call at our Parlors where the process of
Boning will be carefully explained, and instructions given
without charge.

For printed directions apply at the parlors or address

WARREN FEATHERBONE CO.

Patentees and Manufacturers.

THREE OAKS. MICH.

NEW YORK OFFICE, 907 Broadway.
CHICAGO OFFICE, 720 Marshall Field & Co. Building

Dress Boning Parlors :

907 Broadway, New York.
722 Marshall Field & Co. Building,
Chicago.
40 West Street, Boston.
1113 Chestnut Street, Philadelphia.

The accompanying cut
illustrates the use of the

FEATHERBONE TAPES

for collar, cuff and rever
stiffening and our

SLEEVE EXTENDERS

or Duplex Skirt Bone in
sleeves. The smooth effect
of the waist is secured by
stitching our waist bone in
with a sewing machine.

83

The Woman's
❦ Bicycle

In strength, lightness, grace, and elegance of finish and equipment Model 41 Columbia is unapproached by any other make.

Columbia

saddles are recommended by riders and physicians as proper in shape and adjustment, and every detail of equipment contributes to beauty and the comfort and pleasure of the rider.

$100 TO ALL ALIKE.

The Columbia Catalogue, handsomest art work of the year, is free from the Columbia agent, or is mailed by us for two 2-cent stamps.

POPE MFG. CO., Hartford, Conn.

Branch Stores and Agencies in almost every city and town. If Columbias are not properly represented in your vicinity, let us know.

All Columbia Bicycles are fitted with
HARTFORD SINGLE-TUBE TIRES
UNLESS DUNLOP TIRES ARE ASKED FOR.
WE KNOW NO TIRES SO GOOD AS HARTFORDS.